THE VISCOUNT'S CODE

RECKLESS ROGUES
BOOK TWO

ELLIE ST. CLAIR

Facebook: Ellie St. Clair

Cover by AJF Designs

Do you love historical romance? Receive access to a free ebook, as well as exclusive content such as giveaways, contests, freebies and advance notice of pre-orders through my mailing list!

Sign up here!

Reckless Rogues
The Earls's Secret
The Viscount's Code
The Scholar's Key
Prequel, The Duke's Treasure, available in:
I Like Big Dukes and I Cannot Lie

For a full list of all of Ellie's books, please see
www.elliestclair.com/books.

CHAPTER 1

"We cannot welcome that man into our home."

Hope bit her lip, staring up at her sister's set jaw, the hard line of her lips, the steely determination in her eyes.

"We would be doing so to help Cassandra and Gideon, Faith. It is not for ourselves."

Faith turned her stare away from the man in question toward Hope, hands on her hips and a disapproving frown on her face. "One of these days, Hope, you will have to start thinking of yourself instead of everyone else."

Hope sighed as she glanced across the room at Anthony Davenport, Viscount Whitehall. She agreed with her sister – she would rather not welcome to their home a man who had just called their father a thief, even if he hadn't meant for her and Faith to overhear. However, to refuse would not only disappoint one of her closest friends in the world but would also put a stall to this entire treasure hunt.

For that was what it appeared they had embarked upon – willingly or not.

"Hope, there you are." Cassandra stepped between them

and wrapped Hope's hands in her own, a warm smile on her face. "I was never able to properly thank you for all you did to bring Devon and I back together. I'm not sure that I would ever have forgiven him had you not intervened."

Heat crept up Hope's cheeks. "It was nothing, Cassandra, truly. I simply told him the truth."

"But had you not sought him out, the two of us would have been far too hard-headed to ever admit to our faults, I'm sure," Cassandra said, although the look she sent her fiancé's way was nothing but endearing. "You are quite the peacemaker."

Hope simply nodded. Cassandra was correct in that it had taken a great deal of courage for Hope to approach the earl and tell him what her friend had believed of him, but it had been tearing her apart to see Cassandra so distraught over what Hope had been sure was a misunderstanding.

Fortunately, Lord Covington, who was best friends with Cassandra's brother, Gideon, had taken her seriously and repaired their relationship. Along the way, they had led the rest of them on a rather interesting quest which had resulted in not a treasure as expected, but rather a second clue to this puzzle that had begun at the beginning of the summer.

"Cassandra?" Hope asked now, looking around the room. It was not as though this was a great secret, as all ten of them were in on it. There were the five women whose relationship with one another had centered around their interest in reading inappropriate novels and a penchant for brandy, and the five men who, apparently, had created a club in which they sought out daring schemes and pursuits.

"Yes?" Cassandra asked, raising her eyebrows as she pushed a strand of her auburn hair back behind her ear.

"Do you truly believe the viscount is the only man who can solve this code that appears to exist in the latest clue? And are you sure it even *is* a code?"

Cassandra's initial sigh turned into a chuckle. "I am not actually certain of anything – except that the viscount seems quite convinced that the book we found will match a second, and my father was certain that your father possessed an identical volume. Do you think it will be an issue for the viscount to visit your estate?"

"I certainly think so," Faith huffed. "Do you know what he had to say about our father?"

Hope quelled her sister's words with a look, shaking her head slightly. It wouldn't do to upset Cassandra on this day that was supposed to be for her and her soon-to-be husband.

"It will be fine," she said, attempting to smooth it all over. "Our mothers are such good friends. I should see no issue."

"Thank you," Cassandra said, relief evident on her face. "Gideon is so counting on us finding a treasure of value to restore the family's fortunes. He was utterly disappointed when the riddle we found only led to another clue, but at least it was not the end of it." She turned when her name was called from across the room.

"I best go speak to my soon-to-be mother-in-law. Thank you again for helping us in this."

As she walked away, Hope turned to her sister. "Do you see? We cannot disappoint Cassandra."

Faith sighed. "Fine. But if the viscount says anything further untoward about our family, I shall have to tell Father."

Hope cringed. Their father was not a man who many wanted to cross.

"Very well," she said, hoping the viscount would behave himself. He was rather surly, though she hadn't spent much time with him. If he did visit their estate, he would hopefully keep to himself. "Now, what do you suppose we should say to Mother to convince her to invite them?"

"Since you are so keen on this idea, I am sure you shall

come up with something," Faith said primly. "You're always rather good at convincing others to do as you please, are you not?"

"Faith—"

But Faith had walked away to join their friend Madeline, leaving Hope to sigh and make her way alone to her mother. Faith was right. It wouldn't be difficult to put the idea into her mother's mind – she loved to show off Newfield Manor. As it happened, the estate, near the sea at Harwich, was at its very best this time of year. All Hope needed to do was convince her mother that it was her own idea. And as she was currently speaking with Lady Whitehall, it likely wouldn't take much but an innocent comment or two for the women to decide a visit was imperative.

She stole one last glance at the viscount as she walked across the room. He was cantankerous and gruff and rather scared her, though she would never admit it to anyone. Nor would she share her thoughts that he was rather handsome. Suddenly, as though he could sense her gaze, he turned and locked eyes with her – his so hard and unrelenting that she snapped her head back around as quickly as she could, running from him with an "eep!" that she hoped no one else heard.

Cassandra was wrong. She was a coward.

* * *

ANTHONY WATCHED the angelic figure that was Hope Newfield run away from him, just like most women of her ilk were wont to do.

He scared them. He understood that and was fine with it, for he had no time to coddle a woman prone to such emotional theatrics.

If they were different people, however, the things he

could do to cause that pink flush to wash over her face…. He wondered if it would travel over the rest of her body as well.

But that wasn't for him to discover. Besides, if she knew what his family was suspected of, she would want even less to do with him than she already did.

He scoffed as he turned back to Ferrington. The man would one day become a marquess, yet he sailed through life without a care in the world, so opposite to Anthony himself, who felt the weight of it pressing on his shoulders with every step he took.

"You are to go to Newfield House, then?" Ferrington asked him, to which Anthony nodded.

"It appears so – if it can be arranged."

"Interesting," Ferrington mused, taking a sip of his drink and rocking back and forth from his toes to his heels as he looked around the room. "Haven't been there in some time myself."

"Do you have reason to?" Anthony asked, picking up on something in the man's tone.

Ferrington shrugged, although the right side of his lip twitched upward. "I might have a care for a particular person there."

"Oh?" Anthony wasn't altogether interested, but it seemed like the natural progression of the conversation.

Ferrington leaned in. "I know I shouldn't say anything, but Lady Faith has caught my eye."

"Lady Faith?" Anthony choked out. He couldn't see anything particularly attractive about the woman, who did nothing to hide the derision in her gaze every time she looked at him. He had an inkling that she believed the rumors that had followed him around.

"Yes, Lady Faith," Ferrington said dreamily before sighing into his drink. "Unfortunately, she wants nothing to do with me."

"You asked?"

"I did. Well, asked her for a dance once or twice, to walk with me another time. She continues to turn me down."

"Why?"

Ferrington shrugged. "She will not say. She hasn't been known to be courted by any man, however, so I suppose I cannot be overly insulted."

"I see," Anthony murmured, and while he didn't care about Lady Faith's interest in a husband, he wondered if her sister felt the same about suitors. Not that it mattered to him, for he would certainly not be pursuing her.

"So how do you know about solving these codes?" Ferrington asked, changing the subject.

"My father taught me," Anthony said, waiting for the judgment to come, but Ferrington only seemed interested.

"How did he learn them?"

"He was a codebreaker in the war," Anthony said, wishing Ferrington would finish this line of questioning. "He had hoped I would follow him into it, but..." Then all had come crashing down. "The need never arose."

"Right. Well, an interesting skill, if not one that is often required."

"True."

"Who'd have thought Ashford would have need of it in some treasure hunt?" Ferrington continued.

"Who, indeed?"

Anthony had hoped his short answers would discourage Ferrington's questioning, but the man didn't seem affected by his responses at all.

"Well, best go congratulate the new couple," he said with a cheerful smile. "Best of luck with the code! We shall all be waiting to hear how you make out."

Best of luck. Anthony wished he'd kept his mouth shut

when he had recognized the potential of a code in the book they had unearthed. Now they were all counting on him to solve this mystery. And while he had recognized a code existed, he wasn't sure he had any chance of breaking it. He had never been nearly as intelligent as his father, unfortunately. If he was, perhaps he could have cleared his name years ago.

He watched Hope speak to her mother, who was standing with his own. Hope glanced toward him once again, and he could only imagine how much she must be regretting their agreement for him to come visit.

Anthony was rather concerned as well – for the fair Hope with her soft blond hair, her deep blue eyes, and porcelain skin was all he had ever wanted and exactly what he couldn't have. Her beauty made Ferrington's revelation all the more surprising. What was it about Lady *Faith* that would attract a man over her sister?

Every other man he knew was enamoured with Lady Hope – a group he refused to join, as he was far from the man for her.

"Anthony!"

He had been so focused on his ridiculous musings that he hadn't been paying attention to the room around him.

"Yes, Mother?" She was standing by his side.

"Lady Embury has invited us to visit their estate within a fortnight."

His mother was wringing her hands together nervously. He hated how unsure of herself she had become since their father's death and the accusations that had been brought against him.

"Would you like to accept?" he asked, even though he knew he was supposed to be encouraging the visit.

"I am not entirely sure," she said, hedging. "It would be lovely to spend time with Lady Embury. We've been friends since we were girls, of course, and it has been some time since I have been to their country home. It is just…"

"Just what?"

"Since your father died, I haven't quite felt like myself."

Anthony softened at her words, and he reached out and placed a hand on her arm.

"Then perhaps a visit with an old friend is just what you need."

She hesitated before nodding, a small smile flitting across her face for just a moment.

"Perhaps you are right," she said, straightening. "I shall tell Lady Embury we will be there within a week, if you are agreeable."

"I am. I need to return home to see to a few matters, but we are in such close proximity to Newfield Manor, I see no issue."

"Wonderful!" His mother brightened, and Anthony hoped desperately that Lady Embury would be considerate and not raise any topics that would cause his mother's smile to fade. "I shall go inform her of the good news."

Anthony shoved his hands in his pockets, watching her as she returned to Lady Embury, who was standing with Lady Hope herself. Her eyes caught his once more, and he found himself nearly lost in their ocean blue depths.

"Not for me," he murmured to himself, wondering how many times in the coming days he would have to repeat that utterance. "Not for me."

CHAPTER 2

"*Y*ou seem nervous."

"I'm not nervous." Hope crossed her arms over her chest, trying to convince herself as well as her sister that there was nothing to fear. "We shall be spending most of our time with Lady Whitehall, who seems rather lovely."

"She is beside herself."

Hope stopped pacing to look at her sister, who was sitting at her writing desk, pen scratching upon the paper, obviously completely unaffected by their upcoming visitors.

"That is not kind."

"It is the truth," Faith said, flipping to her next page. "The woman can barely speak without seeking approval. It is a wonder that Mother is still friends with her."

"It is hardly a wonder. Mother far prefers friends and acquaintances who will sit still and listen to her instead of trying to interject a word themselves."

"Also true," Faith acknowledged, and Hope couldn't help a small sigh. Faith was actually quite a bit like their mother, although she would never actually *tell* her sister that, for she was sure the comment would be met with derision.

"You do not think anyone will find it odd that the viscount is accompanying his mother?"

"Not with his mother's current state of mind," Faith said. "Now, I am sure Father will have questions as to why the viscount is so interested in spending all of his time with his nose in books."

"Do you think Father will allow him to look at his own book quite readily?"

"I am not sure. I have to admit that I have never seen the book in question, which means that he has it hidden away somewhere. Fortunately, that is not our problem. As the viscount is the one who claims to be able to crack this code, he can be the one to discover the book as well. We promised to arrange the visit. We have lived up to our part of this arrangement."

"We? I do believe you left me to see it through."

"For I would have declined to have anything to do with it," Faith finished with a smile for Hope, who could only sigh once more. She had never won a battle of wills with Faith, and she supposed she likely never would.

"He is not one to talk much, is he?" Hope mused.

"No, although I suppose that is for the best," Faith said, "for whenever he does speak, he only serves to darken the mood of the entire party. Perhaps that is why his mother is so on edge herself."

"Faith! That is not fair. Mother said she has been a different woman since the death of her husband."

"Perhaps."

"You are quite frustrating, do you know that?" Hope said, standing and crossing the small parlor. She had chosen to sit here this morning because it offered a view of the front drive. It was beautiful, yes, with the gardens blooming around the fountain that stood in the middle of the circled path, but it would also allow her to see when their guests arrived.

"I do," Faith said, her voice calling out to Hope as she stood in front of the three large sash windows, the cream curtains pulled back to showcase the outdoors beyond. "Why do you not sit and play for me while we wait? Your nerves are getting to me."

Hope turned around, annoyed with herself that her sister could read her emotions so easily. "What would you have me play?"

"Anything you like, as long as it is not dreary."

As they were in the front room, Hope's harp and pianoforte were not available to her, but her mandolin was sitting upon the side table.

She knew her sister's favorites – she just wondered whether she should play one for her, or if it would be far more fun to vex her with something she hated.

"Play *The Mansion of Peace*, if you will," Faith said, and Hope nodded, unable to decline. Faith was right. She always chose to please others before herself.

She picked at the strings of the mandolin, softly singing the words to accompany the song as she stared out the window, anticipation heavy in her breast.

What was it about the viscount that bothered her so? And just what was she going to do about it?

She saw the horses first as they rounded the bend and started up the drive. She stopped playing so abruptly that Faith's head snapped up to her, and heat crept into Hope's cheeks.

"What has gotten into you?" Faith asked, horrified. "It is not as though we have never had a visitor before." She paused, staring at her. "You are not *taken* with the viscount, are you?"

"Of course not!" Hope said crossly. "Not only is he far from affable, but I will never accept a suitor until you do."

"That is ridiculous," Faith said, waving her hand. "I am never going to have a suitor, so do not hold yourself to that. I would far rather you find a man who will make you happy. That will make *me* happy in turn."

"But, Faith—"

"Do not wait for me, Hope," Faith said, shaking her head before pursing her lips. "I ask only that you promise me one thing."

"What is it?"

"Do not allow the viscount to be that man for you."

"Of course not. But I'm curious – why?" Hope asked, curious.

"You will just have to trust me," Faith said crisply. "Now, let us go prepare for our visitors."

* * *

A STRANGE SENSATION that he was being watched tugged on Anthony's spine as he held his hand out to help his mother down from the carriage on the front drive of the stately Newfield Manor which rose before him.

He knew how proud the Emburys were of their country home, which was currently working to his advantage as Lady Embury was keen to invite visitors to show it off.

"It's beautiful, isn't it?" his mother asked wistfully, following his gaze.

"So is Whitehall Manor, Mother," he said, and she nodded, although her face was drawn. A forced smile emerged, however, when a voice cut through the fresh spring air of the day.

"Lady Whitehall! So good to see you."

Lady Embury was standing at the top of the stairs, her

arms open to welcome them. Anthony's mother took his elbow, and he led her up to greet their hosts. Anthony nodded at his own welcome before stepping back, and soon noted Lord Embury standing behind them in the entrance. His bearded jowls were set into a scowl as he looked from Anthony to his mother and back again, and Anthony stiffened in response, although he refused to allow the man to see how he affected him.

"Lord Embury," he said, reaching a hand out, and the man was too well-bred to refuse as he took it in a quick, firm shake.

"Thank you for inviting us, my lord," Anthony said, but the earl simply nodded, which Anthony took as confirmation that he'd had no choice in the matter.

Anthony looked around for a glimpse of the ladies Hope and Faith, but they seemed suspiciously absent.

"My daughters are also looking forward to welcoming you," Lady Embury said as though she had read his thoughts, although a quick glance at her husband suggested that perhaps he hadn't been interested in having them greet Anthony and his mother. "They are currently taking their luncheon. Are you hungry yourselves?"

"Not at the moment," Anthony's mother said. "Perhaps we will retire to our rooms for a rest before we dine."

"Very well," Lady Embury said, lifting her arm out to motion to the few servants who had gathered behind them, prepared for their arrival. "My staff will look after you. Why do we not meet in the drawing room tonight at seven o'clock? Until then, please feel free to make the estate your own."

"Thank you," Anthony's mother said, and, while he was currently famished, he had no choice but to follow her lead. She seemed rather peaked, and once he saw her settled, he decided to take himself on a tour of the house, even though he had been in residence but a month before when Lord and Lady Embury had hosted a ball to begin the summer season.

He was walking through the great hall, colorful sunbeams reaching through the mosaic of stained-glass windows above, when he heard soft notes of music filtering through the rooms. Was it one of the ladies, he wondered? He told himself that he should walk the other way and not be drawn to it like a rat to the pied piper, but there was something so hauntingly beautiful about the music that his feet seemed to have a mind of their own as they followed the notes through the hall.

The closer he walked to the back of the house, the louder the music became, and the clearer he could hear the sweet melodic voice that accompanied it.

He finally stopped in the doorway of a music room, and there, sitting across from him at the pianoforte, was the enchanting figure of Lady Hope. Her back was to him, and he knew he should likely make his presence known instead of standing there staring at her like a voyeur, but he was too caught in her spell that continued to weave around him with every note she played and every word she sang.

"Dawn breaks and sweet birds sing, a symphony of joy on the wind."

Anthony had no idea how long he stood there, as a longing deep within him urged him to open his mouth and join her, but it had been so long since he had played or sang any type of music, a gift his father had passed down to him, that he wondered if he would even remember how.

Then she stopped so abruptly that he jolted upright, and it seemed as though his soul was settling itself back into his body.

He froze, unsure if he should make his escape before alerting her to his presence, but when she turned her head to the side as though sensing him, he knew it was too late.

"Lord Whitehall?" she said, standing so quickly that her stool began tipping over behind her. Anthony started across the room to catch it, but as he attempted to make it in time, he tripped over his own feet and went flying toward her instead.

"Oh, no!" Hope cried, and instead of backing away and allowing him to fall, she reached out as though to catch him. Between her own attempt and his last-minute ability to right himself, they both remained standing, but had somehow become locked in an embrace.

When he finally regained his bearings, Anthony looked down, only to find her face inches away from his, her eyes boring into him, her lips rosy, pert, and upturned.

The perfect gift – and one that he must refuse.

"Apologies," he murmured gruffly, and while he knew he should step back, while he'd had the resolve to keep from kissing her, he didn't seem to have it within him to move away from her.

She kept her hands lightly on his arms, and Anthony didn't think he had ever been so warm and comfortable in his life.

That was, until he heard a throat clearing from the doorway and he whipped his head around to find Lady Faith standing there, arms crossed, hip against the edge of the door.

"Well, well," she said. "If it isn't Lord Whitehall. I do suggest you take your hands off my sister."

CHAPTER 3

*G*oodness, what was she doing?

"My apologies, Lord Whitehall," Hope said, stepping backward hastily, only she was so close to the pianoforte that her bottom hit the keys, creating a loud crashing of sound that made her wince. "I am glad you are not hurt."

"And just how would Lord Whitehall hurt himself in a music room?" Faith asked, an eyebrow raised as she peered at the two of them.

"He tripped," Hope said when it appeared that the viscount was not going to explain himself.

"Did my sister's music so captivate you that you could not walk straight?" Faith asked, sarcasm lacing her tone. Hope's face warmed as she saw the viscount's expression harden, and she wondered herself at what had caused his clumsiness.

How long had he been standing there, listening to her? She had been playing a song of her own creation, one that was playful, light, written with the thought of flitting about the gardens on a warm summer's day.

The truth was, once she had seen the viscount's carriage

arrive, she had thought to greet the man and his mother, but her father had told her that the guests were not here to visit her, and that she and Faith could make themselves scarce until dinner. When she had tried to suggest otherwise, she had detected the warning in his tone and did as he bid, but she wondered at it. Just what did he – and Faith – have against the man?

"You are an accomplished musician," the viscount said to Hope, ignoring Faith, but it was Faith who answered before Hope had a chance.

"Of course she is. Hope is perfection at nearly everything she attempts."

"That is not at all true," Hope said hastily. While she did pick up young lady's accomplishments rather easily, she was not nearly as intelligent as Faith. She also never seemed to know the right thing to say in many circumstances and had no wit or humor. Not that she was going to spell out all of her faults to the viscount at the moment.

"I assure you it is," Faith said, and Hope wondered at the bit of malice that laced her tone. She sent a concerned, questioning look at Faith, but she ignored her.

"Since we have a moment alone," Lord Whitehall said, looking from Hope to Faith and back again, "I thought I might ask a favour."

"Of course," Faith and Hope both said at the same time, except that Hope meant what she said while Faith was obviously not quite as sincere.

"This book that I am to examine – have you seen it?"

"No," Hope said, biting her lip. "Unfortunately, we have not. In fact, I do not recall *ever* seeing such a book. As hopeful as I am that we can locate it, I do wonder at the duke's memory."

Cassandra's father, the Duke of Ashford, had been the one to recall that Hope's father possessed a similar edition to the

17

one they had found after following the riddle. His Grace, however, suffered a disease of the mind that could bring his reliability into question.

"I find that when it is the past in question, His Grace is usually correct," the viscount said, rubbing a hand over his brow. "Where do you suppose I should look?"

"Likely his study," Hope said. "Although perhaps we should simply *ask* Father."

"No," Faith interjected swiftly. "I do not think he would be in favour of the idea."

"Why not?" Hope asked.

Faith looked over to the viscount. "He is not Lord White-hall's biggest admirer."

"Faith!" Hope exclaimed, her eyes shooting over to Lord Whitehall, who smirked.

"I am not shocked," he said.

"Does our father know you well?" Hope asked, to which Lord Whitehall shook his head.

"No."

"Then why—"

"He knew my father."

Hope looked back and forth from Faith's hard expression to Lord Whitehall's, knowing she was missing something, but it seemed that neither of them was inclined to share at the moment.

"Very well," she said, raising her hands in the air. "I think, however, you are best to simply ask Father. Perhaps he will be reasonable."

Faith snorted at that, and Hope shot a look her way. Was she the only one who actually wanted to get to the bottom of this and help her friends?

"Best of luck, my lord," Faith said with an amused smile. "Come, Hope, we best prepare for dinner."

"But—"

Before Hope could finish her sentence, Faith had taken her arm and was practically pulling her out the door. Hope took one look back at the viscount, whose lips were set in a grim line. She had a feeling that this visit was not going to end well. She just had no idea why that would be.

* * *

DINNER SEEMED TO TAKE HOURS, but it was likely only because they all spent the entirety of it eating in silence – except for Lady Embury. For Lady Embury talked. And talked. And talked some more. Anthony wondered how she managed to eat at all, as her mouth never seemed to be free for a bite.

At least his mother seemed happy. As much as Lady Embury could be a trial, his mother had always enjoyed her company – perhaps because his mother so abhorred silence herself, even though she seemed to have lost the ability to fill it. He supposed they were a perfect match as friends, and he told himself that if nothing else, he was glad to bring his mother some peace.

After dinner, the women retired to the drawing room, and Lord Embury begrudgingly offered him a drink when they remained seated at the table. Anthony accepted, primarily because he could see no better opportunity to speak with Lord Embury about the book.

"Tell me, Whitehall," Lord Embury said, leaning back in his chair, his thick white eyebrows lowering over his eyes, "Why did you accompany your mother here to Newfield Manor?"

Anthony chose his words carefully. "My mother has been... fragile since the passing of my father," he said. "She was most excited about this visit, but I thought it best that she not come alone."

"I see," Lord Embury said, steepling his fingers together. "And this has nothing to do with my daughters?"

Did he know of their quest?

"I am not sure what you mean."

"You are not interested in making a match with one of them?"

"No."

Now the earl's eyebrows shot up to the top of his forehead. "And why not? Do you find fault with them?"

Anthony had to restrain himself from rolling his eyes at the man. Just what was he after?

"No. I am not interested in marrying."

Not until he had cleared his family's name.

"That is an odd statement."

Anthony shrugged. He had nothing to prove to the viscount.

"I do not know what your aim is here, Whitehall, but you must know one thing."

Anthony waited.

"Stay away from my daughters."

Anthony mocked the man – although he likely didn't even realize what he was doing – by winging up one eyebrow himself in question.

"They are good girls," Lord Embury said with pride, "and I am looking to make a strong match for both of them."

"I am a viscount," Anthony said, riling the man, waiting for him to say what Anthony knew he was thinking – that he may be a viscount but that he was from a tainted line.

"Thought you weren't interested."

"I'm not."

Now they were going around in circles. Time to get on with it.

"I do have a question for you," Anthony began, leaning forward.

"Here we are. What is it?"

Anthony smiled, but it was a grim one. "I am looking for a book."

"You'll have to be more specific. I have an entire library full of them."

"Very well. It is a brown leather-bound book in hand-written scrawl."

He waited for the earl's reaction, but he gave away nothing, except for the slightest tick of his right eye.

"What's so special about this book?"

Anthony hadn't been sure how much he would share with the man, and decided to tell a half-truth, as he didn't feel that he could yet trust him – or if he would ever be able to.

"I am a book collector. I have found one similar and I would like to compare it to yours."

"Why would you think I have such a book?"

"I heard a rumor."

That would teach the earl about rumors.

"Whatever rumor you heard is false," Embury said, sitting back in his chair, crossing his arms over his chest.

"So you have never heard of such a book?"

"I have not."

"That is too bad," Anthony mused.

"I suppose you have come all of this way for nothing, then," the earl said now, and Anthony shrugged.

"That's not true. I also have the wonderful company of your family."

He smiled coldly at the man, then, knowing how much his words likely irked him. It was not that he had anything against Embury. He just didn't like how the earl was treating him, as though he was someone lesser than – not good enough for his daughters, clearly suspicious about his motives. Anthony could tell he had the book in his possession. He just didn't want to share it with him, likely convinced that he was a traitor, if he believed the same about Anthony's own father.

"Be careful, son," Lord Embury said, eyeing him, to which Anthony stood.

"I am not your son," he said, biting out the words, before motioning toward the door. "Perhaps we should go join the women now."

"Perhaps," Lord Embury said. "Remember what I said about my daughters."

"How could I forget?" Anthony murmured.

As much as Anthony was pleased to be away from Lord Embury and his judging stare, when they entered the drawing room, he immediately regretted his suggestion, for Lady Embury's incessant chatter hadn't ebbed since they had retired. One would think she would have run out of topics by now.

She paused for a moment and greeted the men when they entered before she returned to her soliloquy on whatever it was that most noblewomen amused themselves with – for this particular woman it seemed to be the latest gossip of the day. Lady Embury was quite proud of her letter writing and had much to share from it.

When she finally took a breath, Anthony interjected. "Excuse me."

Lady Embury looked to him as if he had interrupted the Prince Regent himself.

"Yes, Lord Whitehall?"

"Perhaps one of the young ladies could play a song for us."

Lady Embury's eyelashes fluttered as she brought a hand to her chest and Anthony gathered that, if she was anything like most noble mothers of young ladies, she was as interested in showing off her daughters as she was in gossiping about their rivals. "Oh. Well, I suppose."

A smile lit the face of Anthony's mother. She had always

loved music, particularly when his father had played, and had been asking him to take up instruments for a time now. He had always refused.

"Anthony has always loved music," she said softly, and he nodded stiffly. At this point, anything was better than listening to Lady Embury.

"Faith, would you like to play?" Hope asked now giving cause for Anthony to look over at where she sat in the corner, her hands folded demurely in her lap.

"Of course not," Faith said with a frown. "You should."

"Very well," Hope said, standing and running her hands down the soft muslin of her pale blue skirts as she walked over to the pianoforte in the corner.

Then she sat, removed her gloves from her long, slender fingers, and began to play.

It was like magic filled the air, as Anthony never wanted her to stop.

And for the first time, in a long time, he felt completely at peace.

CHAPTER 4

*W*hen Hope's father and Lord Whitehall joined them in the drawing room, Hope hadn't missed the tension that had followed them in. It was so thick; she almost wouldn't have been surprised if they told her they had come to blows.

Which was why, when she had sat at the pianoforte as shockingly requested by the viscount, she had picked the brightest, cheeriest song she could possibly think of, one which had even brought a smile to Faith's face, despite the fact that her sister wasn't pleased about having to accompany Hope on the mandolin.

While Faith enjoyed listening to Hope's music, she hated playing as much as Hope loved it.

Hope had been surprised by Lady Whitehall's declaration that her son was a musician himself – she wouldn't have guessed it, but then, what did she expect of the man, that he sat in his house brooding all day?

As she'd played, her mind had wandered, and hadn't been able to help but wonder if the tension between the men had been caused by a discussion about the book that Lord Whitehall was here to find and study. Had he asked her father about it? It only made sense. Which was why Hope determined that she would solve this problem herself. It was the only way to keep the peace among everyone else.

They had all retired over an hour ago – mercifully earlier than usual, after the interminable chatter in the drawing room – and Hope had waited until she could no longer hear anyone walking about to let herself out of her bedroom. Instead of going directly to her destination, she followed the corridor the other way, pausing outside of her parents' bedrooms. She placed her ear against her father's door, pleased when she heard her mother prattling away. Her mother may have been in her own room, but her voice was loud enough that it carried through the open doorway into her father's chamber. All were abed for the night, then.

Hope tiptoed down the hall, her slippers barely making a sound on the thick carpet that ran over the wood flooring. If she were her father, where would she keep a book of significance? She ignored the other question, the one that bothered her – *why* would her father keep such a book hidden? If the duke recalled seeing the book here, why wouldn't her father have wanted to share its secrets with her and Faith?

She paused in front of the library, peeking into the dark room, but quickly disregarded it. Her father would not have hidden a book he wanted to keep secret in a public room. It had to be his study. He spent a great deal of time in there alone, and at no time would anyone – besides a maid – be in there without her father present.

Hope stopped in front of the room at the end of the corridor, which was nestled in the back corner of the estate. The doors were shut but unlocked, and as she pushed them open, the scent of her father – cheroot smoke and leather with a hint of musty books – washed over her. Only embers smoldered in the fireplace, and she pulled her wrapper tighter around herself to ward against the chill. She'd had no choice but to change into her nightclothes, as her maid would have been suspicious if she stayed dressed in her dinner clothes.

The dark curtains were drawn, hiding the moonlight, and Hope lifted her candle, raising it to the bookshelves across from her father's desk. Would he have hidden it here in plain sight? she wondered, concentrating on the titles in front of her.

She was so focused on her task that she didn't hear a noise from the hall beyond – until a voice sounded right behind her ear.

"Boo."

"Ah!" Hope exclaimed, her voice just below a scream, startled as she was by the unexpected presence. She whirled around to find the viscount standing there behind her, his arms crossed with a smirk on his face.

"Do you continue to do this to me on purpose?"

"I am not to blame for your inability to observe the room around you."

"In one day, you have twice come upon me unexpectedly."

"Except that it is now tomorrow."

"Let us not make a habit of doing this once per day."

Then the surly viscount, the man who never smiled and barely ever spoke, did something even more surprising. He laughed.

It was not a full-bodied laugh of joy, but it was a chuckle. And the true smile on his face nearly astonished her, for, while she had always silently appreciated his dark features that matched his broody demeanor, his smile made him downright handsome.

For a moment, she couldn't find any words.

"Have you found anything?" he asked, the moment having passed, and Hope cleared her throat, turning away, hoping that he hadn't noticed how affected she was by him.

"No," she said, shaking her head. "I am assuming that you asked my father about the book?"

"I did."

"And?" Did the man *ever* elaborate when asked a question?

"And he told me that I must have been mistaken, that he had never heard of such a book."

Hope frowned, biting her lip. "Why would he lie?"

"Could be that he actually doesn't have the book. Which I doubt. Could be that he doesn't *want* to admit he has it, because it is stolen. Or it could be that he doesn't trust me."

Ire simmered in Hope's belly at his words. "Why would you think the book is stolen?"

"Because of what was in the riddle – the books should have been found together. But instead, one was missing. I'm sure it wasn't given to your family."

"So instead, you assume my father stole it?"

"Not necessarily your father. Could have been his father."

"We have no idea what the circumstances were that led to the book being in his possession. I hardly think labelling either my father or one of my ancestors a thief is fair."

Hope clenched her hands into fists, the unfamiliar anger growing within her. The nerve of the man. She wished she had never noticed his handsomeness, for he didn't deserve any attention, as far as she was concerned.

He eyed her as though she was a naïve idiot, which she didn't appreciate. People had underestimated her all her life. She didn't need to add Lord Whitehall to that list.

"So why are you looking for the book, then, so late at night once everyone is abed?" he asked, lifting a brow as well as his lantern in front of the book shelf, peering at the titles with her.

Hope bristled. She hadn't prepared a response, for she wouldn't have guessed that she would have need to answer him tonight.

27

"I thought it would be easiest to look myself first," she said primly. "If I do not find it tonight, then I will ask my father tomorrow."

"If you ask him, you will have to explain all of it," he said. "He would be suspect if we both asked for the same book within a day of one another."

"That is true," she acknowledged. "Why do we not decide on the best course of action if it should prove necessary?"

He nodded. "Very well."

She turned from him, and they worked in silence for a time, perusing the book shelf, looking for both the title and the correct size and shape of the book, in case it was hidden. When they finished without their search having come to fruition, the viscount stepped away and over to the desk.

"Could it be in here?"

Hope had thought of that, but she didn't like the idea of a practical stranger searching within the desk.

"It could but I do not feel right about looking within. My father wouldn't like it."

"Then he should have given me the book," Lord Whitehall said, leaning over and running his hands along the desk. Instead of going around to the drawers, however, he was studying the back of the desk.

"What are you doing?" she asked, crouching beside him.

"I am trying to determine if there are any secret drawers or compartments back here," he said, before peering closer at it. "Wait a minute," he murmured, and Hope frowned and followed the path of his fingers.

"What is it?"

"Beneath the desk," he said, so focused on his task that it seemed as though he was nearly talking to himself instead of to her. "There are small panels that I can pull out."

He caught a piece beneath the lip of the desk, pulling it out in front of him. It had small notches on it that looked to be numbers. "There are four of them," he said, his eyes wide. "I wonder…"

"You wonder what?" Hope said, wanting to shake him, wishing he would just talk plainly to her.

"I wonder if it is some kind of code, if the right combination of numbers would open a secret part of the desk."

"That is absurd."

He looked at her, his eyes brighter than she had seen them before, and she realized that he was excited about this – as excited as Lord Whitehall seemed to get about anything.

"So is a riddle and the thought that a code could lead to treasure," he said.

Hope could only sigh in defeat. "I suppose that is true."

"What do you suppose the code might be?" he asked, looking at her, and for the first time Hope saw the color of his eyes – a dark grey that reminded her of a storm cloud, one that threatened rain showers but also brought with it the fresh smell that promised a green beauty to follow.

"P-pardon?" she said, forgetting his question.

His lips firmed into a line, and she was aware that he was a rather impatient man, but what was to be expected when he stared at her with such intensity?

"I asked what you thought the numbers might be. It's your father's desk. It would likely be something meaningful to him."

"It could be," she said, rubbing her forehead distractedly as she thought. "Unless, as you say, it was not he who hid the book."

"Did you know your grandfather well?" he asked, and Hope shook her head.

"No. He was always rather distracted, never spent much time with us, as would be expected, for we were so young. I did, however, know my grandmother."

"Were she and your grandfather a love match?"

"I am not certain, actually."

"What would have meaning, then?"

Hope paced around the room. "The year of her birth? The year they were wed? The year my father was born?"

Lord Whitehall nodded. "Let's try the latter. It is what every nobleman wants, is it not? A son?"

"Is that what you want?" she surprised herself by asking, as much as she obviously equally shocked him.

"Let's stay on topic."

"Very well," she said, her face warming in embarrassment. "1760."

Hope watched, fascinated, as he lay down on his back under the desk, reaching up and sliding a panel forward. She was so intrigued, she couldn't help herself from lying down on the floor next to him. He turned his head to the side to stare at her for a moment, his face but a breath away from hers, before turning back to his task.

He slid the next panel forward, and Hope couldn't help but watch his hands with fascination. He had long, strong fingers, ones that did remind her of a musician's.

She waited, not realizing for a moment that she was holding her breath, until she nearly gasped in need of it.

Finally, he slid the last panel open, and a whirring sound arose, followed by a click.

They had done it.

CHAPTER 5

nthony felt the rare thrill of elation wash through him when he heard the click.

They had guessed right. And now the desk was going to reveal to them exactly what he was looking for.

He turned to look at Hope, seeing an equally enthralled expression on her face, and they shared a smile of triumphant joy. He was so captivated by her angelic face that he nearly forgot what they had just achieved – until he heard the thunk, and he scrambled out from underneath the desk to find a panel had opened on the side of it, revealing a hidden chamber – and the book he had been looking for.

"Here it is," he said in wonder.

"That was a great amount of effort to hide a book," Hope said in amazement, coming to stand beside him as he reached down and picked up the desk's offering.

"You're right about that," he said, placing the book upon the desk, folding it open, dusting the pages reverently.

"Is this the one we were looking for?" she asked, and he nodded.

"It is the companion copy to the book we found in Castleton's stables," he said. "I think with the letter that accompanied it, I should be able to determine from the pages where to look within it. We won't know for certain if I am correct until I begin to work on the code and we see whether anything intelligible comes from it."

"I'm sure you can do it," she murmured.

He was surprised at her faith in him but accepted it, nonetheless. She was such a quiet presence, and he found that she calmed him when she was near. She brought peace with her, whether it was through saying the right thing, saying nothing at all, or even playing music, as she had last night. Unlike her mother – or her sister – she didn't speak unless it was necessary, and when she did, it was always in such a serene manner, even if the subject was tense.

His gaze lifted from the book, locked on her instead.

"Hope," he began, his voice husky, and she looked up at him, her lids blinking over those beautiful blue eyes.

"Yes?"

The truth was, he didn't know what he was going to say. He just knew that he wanted to continue to have a reason to keep her here with him, for her to think something – anything – about him besides that he was a surly man with a traitor of a father.

"I—"

"What is the meaning of this?"

They turned as one to the anger in the doorway, and Anthony's heart sank when he saw the earl standing there, his feet planted, his arms over his chest, his entire body vibrating in his anger.

"Good evening, Father," Hope said from beside Anthony, and as she slightly tremored against his arm, he felt the need to reach out and pull her in next to him.

But of course, in his rational mind, he knew that would do nothing but stoke her father's temper.

"Good evening?" her father repeated, his low voice gruff and angry. "It is not the dinner hour, Hope. It is well past midnight." He looked between the two of them, rage simmering in his voice; however, the fact that he kept it quiet and even actually scared Anthony more than if he were bellowing at them.

Not that anything ever truly scared Anthony.

"You are both well-bred enough to be aware that your presence here – alone – at this time of night should cause Hope to be compromised." He drew a visibly deep breath, obviously calming himself. "However. As I am the only one aware of this… indiscretion, I am willing to overlook it and forget about it – as long as the two of you do as well. Understand?"

Hope nodded, as did Anthony, even as a piece of him was filled with disappointment that the man would think so little of him that he would not even force him to make good on the situation.

"You are being very rational about this, Father," Hope said, surprise in her voice, and her father then turned a dark gaze onto Anthony.

"It is because I would rather see you ruined then married to a traitor."

"Father!" Hope gasped.

"Now see here," Anthony said, standing straight, pride filling him, causing him to lose rational thought. "I am no traitor."

"Your father was," the earl said now, entering the room completely.

"That is a lie!" Anthony returned, stepping toward him.

"You cannot prove that."

"But I will," Anthony seethed.

"Do what you want. I do not care," the earl said. "But I

will not have my daughter married off to you, compromised or not."

"I will prove you wrong," Anthony said, his fingernails biting into his palms, as he slowly came back to his body and realized that he and the earl were standing toe-to-toe, as near to blows as he had ever come with a nobleman his senior.

"It sounds like there has been a misunderstanding," Hope said, standing and holding out one of her hands to each of them. "And now is not the time to return to the past, except to assure you that nothing untoward occurred between me and Lord Whitehall, and I think we are all in agreement that we may continue on."

"Very well," the earl said, bringing his fingers to his temples and stepping backward. "Now, we should all retire, as—"

He stopped, and Anthony followed the earl's gaze, which now rested on the book. Apparently, he hadn't realized what they had been doing here until this moment.

"Father, we can explain," Hope said, lifting her hands up in front of her, and the look that the earl now pinned on Anthony was nearly murderous.

"When I told you I didn't have the book, you should have dropped the subject entirely. I do not know how you ever found it, but it was not your place to even search for it."

"It wasn't his fault," Hope said, stepping forward, and while Anthony didn't require her to protect him, he was actually rather touched by her attempt. "I was the one who came down looking for it."

"We both did, actually, my lord. This was not a prearranged meeting but rather one of happenstance, as we were both searching it out."

"Hope," the earl said, turning to her, and Anthony was

surprised by the hurt in his eyes. "Why would you betray me like this?"

"Father, I didn't mean to do so," she said, desperation lacing her tone, and Anthony was aware how much she loathed to hurt anyone else – likely most especially anyone within her family. "It is just that the book means a great deal to very dear friends of mine, and I wanted to see if I could locate it myself before asking you and upsetting you about it."

"I can assure you this is far worse."

"I see that now," Hope said, her head lowering. "Why do we not sit down, and I will explain all?"

Her father paused for a moment as though he might say no, until he nodded reluctantly and waved them to the table in the corner, each of them taking a chair around it. Anthony felt the brunt of the earl's glare again and knew he would likely be taking most of the blame for this, but he was willing to do so if this ended as he hoped.

"You see, Father, this all began with a riddle," Hope said, her fingers winding around one another. Anthony wasn't sure that they should be explaining all, but it wasn't for him to stop Hope from sharing what she wished with her father. "Gideon and Cassandra discovered the riddle in some of their ancestors' possessions. It appears it was the beginning of something of a treasure hunt. Cassandra and Devon – another long story – eventually discovered that the riddle led to a book, which they found at Castleton."

"How does this relate to *my* book?" Lord Embury asked, crossing his arms over his chest.

"The book we found matches this one," she said, sitting forward earnestly, her eyes lighting up as she explained. "The duke said he recalled the twin at our house."

"The duke?" Lord Embury repeated. "The Duke of Sheffield?"

"Yes."

The earl gave a dismissive wave of his hand. "The man can barely remember his own name."

Hope leaned in, looking squarely at her father. She might prefer to keep the peace, but she also knew when to stand her ground.

"Well, it seems he was right, was he not?"

The earl said nothing for a moment, pausing to stare at first Hope and then Anthony before he sighed in resignation.

"Very well. Obviously, I have the book you asked about. The Duke and I did discover it when we were children, which led my father to hide it."

"How did he come to have it, Father?" Hope asked, for which Anthony was glad, as his own curiosity was also niggling at him but the question was best to come from Hope instead of him.

"It was originally in my grandparents' possession. My grandmother said it belonged to a friend of hers."

Hope and Anthony exchanged a glance. "Perhaps Cassandra's grandmother?" Hope questioned.

"The former duchess? Could be," the earl mused with a distracted nod. "My grandparents instructed my father, who passed on the role to me, to keep it safe. I knew it was there, but I have never known much about it. I was told not to give it to anyone except someone I trusted, someone who had the right message."

"What message would that be?" Anthony asked.

"Why – do you have it?"

"Would it perhaps be…" Anthony closed his eyes to recall the words to his memory. He had them written on a paper in his room, but he could see them in his mind without looking for it. "*Dear friend, it was wonderful to see you again. I have no news to report. Hoping to spend time with you when I visit this summer. Yours, friend.*"

The earl blinked twice. "That's it. This is all rather... sudden, I must say, after years of secrecy. I had nearly forgotten about it until you asked about a book."

"I suppose the time is right," Hope said brightly, although the tension in the room didn't ease.

"What are you proposing to do with my book now?" Lord Embury asked.

"Ideally, I would return home and use it to break the code," Anthony said, but he knew what the earl's answer would be before he even finished his sentence.

"Absolutely not."

"But, Father—"

"I said no." The earl shook his head decisively. "I have kept that book safe for twenty years. I will not have it leaving my possession now – especially with you." He paused for a moment, and Anthony kept silent as he could tell the earl was deep in thought. "You can study it in the library each day you are here," he said, obviously not even happy with his concession. "That will have to do."

Anthony would have liked to argue his point, but he knew that, for now at least, he'd have to be satisfied with what the earl decided to allow.

"Very well," he said. "I'd like to begin tonight." He worked best at night, as it happened.

"It's after midnight!" Lord Embury said with a snort. "Tomorrow."

"I will help," Hope offered.

Her father fixed her with a dark look. "Let Lord White-hall do what he wishes, Hope," he said. "But you will keep to your usual activities."

Hope opened her mouth, likely to argue, but Anthony gave her a nearly imperceptible shake of his head. For one, he didn't need her, and to have her present while he was trying to break a code would only distract him. Second, to push her father too hard would likely only make him take back what he had already promised.

"Very well," Hope said softly, dropping her hands. "Good-night, Father. Lord Whitehall."

Anthony only nodded, watching her rise and walk away. Her father motioned him out of his study before shutting the doors firmly behind him, then followed Anthony up the stairs.

One thing was for certain. This was going to be a long visit.

CHAPTER 6

*H*ope knew she had to be careful, but she couldn't help being drawn to the library. Whether it was the book or the viscount himself that enticed her, she couldn't be certain, nor did she want to clearly make the distinction. For she didn't entirely know what was wrong with her that a man like the viscount intrigued her. Perhaps it was just that she hadn't spent a great deal of time around men such as he – nor had she spent time in the company of any young men in particular, aside from social functions. Her time at Castleton had been the most she had ever spent in the presence of young lords.

She could admit that she was greatly interested in the thought of solving another clue, especially if it meant breaking a code. It made her feel like she was doing something worthwhile, if she was being honest, even if she knew it was nothing more than a silly treasure hunt.

Hope was like a stealthy spy as she all but tiptoed down the corridor. It was not that she was trying to trick her father or go behind his back, it was only that she didn't understand why he would forbid her from being in the presence of the viscount, nor seeing the book. She was sure he would never have forbidden Faith from such a thing – he had much more trust in her actions.

Speaking of Faith… Hope had seen her sister head for the gardens, most likely to practice her archery. She was quite taken with the sport, even though it was only for leisure. Hope tried to tell herself that she hadn't purposely waited for this opportunity to walk past the library – it just happened to be that, while Faith was occupied, she had nothing to do.

Hope entered the library, pretending she was looking for a book on one of the shelves near the entrance – even though she could sense the viscount's presence the moment she walked through the door.

"Lord Whitehall," she said, glancing sideways in his direction as she plucked a book off the shelf at random. "How are you today?"

"Fine," he said without looking up at her. The two leather-bound books were laid out on the table before him. "And you?"

"I am well," she said, smiling at the polite wording of his greeting in his surly gruff voice. She tapped the book against her hand as she walked toward him.

"You are not supposed to be in here," he said, finally lifting his head.

"I am not supposed to spend time with you or with the book," she said. "But I needed something to read, and this is the library, after all."

"It is, isn't it?" The corner of his mouth crooked upward, and when he bent his head slightly, she realized he was looking at the book in her hands.

"Interested in sheep?"

"Sheep?" she repeated.

He gestured toward her. "Your book."

She turned it over, looking at the cover for the first time. "Oh." *Shepherding the Herd.* "Yes, I suppose I am."

He made a noise that sounded like a snort, but Hope realized it was actually something akin to a laugh.

"Thought you read those scandalous books," he commented dryly.

Hope opened her eyes as wide as she could, but his smirk told her that he wasn't buying her shocked innocence.

"How do you know about those?" she asked in a hushed voice instead.

"I have eyes. And with five copies of the book floating about Castleton while we were visiting, I was bound to see one. Didn't take a codebreaker to figure out who was reading them."

Hope's cheeks warmed, but at least she wasn't alone in her embarrassment. Her friends were equally culpable.

"How is the code breaking coming?" she asked, desperately attempting to change the subject, and fortunately, he allowed her to do so.

"Fine. I've not gotten far but have found something of interest."

Hope waited, noticing the viscount glance toward the doorway, likely determining whether her father was about. Little did he know that Faith was the one he should be most worried about.

She stepped closer to him, leaning over his shoulder for a better view of his work, but instead noted how silky his dark hair looked, and she had to stem a strange, irresistible urge to run her fingers through it. He cleared his throat as though he was the one affected, before he pointed to the books in front of her. They appeared to be open to different pages, each containing both text and images. He ran white-gloved fingers gently over each book.

"Be sure not to touch the pages, as they are rather fine

41

and delicate," he said. "Oils from your hands could mar them."

"Very well," she said. "What have you found?"

"The books have the same title, and were obviously created by the same printer, though a rudimentary one, of course, given their age," he said. It appeared he could speak in longer sentences as long as it pertained to a subject of interest to him. "However, they are not the same book, despite their similar appearance."

"What do you mean?" Hope asked, leaning down closer so that she could better see the pages.

"Look," he said. "I have them both open to page 35; however, they contain different text and images. It is that way throughout the books."

"This is to be fiction, is it not?" she asked.

"It is," he said. "As I said, I am just beginning, but from what I can tell, it appears that they are two volumes, comprising one story."

"I see," she breathed. "So my father's copy, which volume was that?"

"The second."

"Have you determined how they might pertain to the code?"

"Not yet. It has something to do with the message included in the first book. Two of the words are underlined, and I have been looking through the book to try to determine what they could mean."

"Can I see?" Hope asked, intrigued now. She pulled up one of the hardbacked chairs next to where he sat behind the writing desk in the corner of the library, beside a window overlooking the green beyond. Fortunately, they were hidden from the door behind a bookshelf, so they would only be seen if someone happened to actually enter the library – which was entirely possible, but she had no interest in leaving now.

He said nothing but pulled out the note and put it on the table in front of her.

She had read it before, but reviewed it again, noting that *summer* and *cordially* were underlined.

She tapped a finger against her lips. "The book is in English, but tells a Spanish story, does it not?"

"Correct."

"And you believe if you find the words within the book, it might help you determine how to decipher the code?"

"That is my hope," he said, and she heard worry in his voice – the first time she had ever seen a vulnerable crack in the armor he wore.

"Why do I not help you? Then it would go faster."

"I believe you were warned not to spend time with me."

"I was."

"Are you not a woman who does as is expected of her?"

"Usually, yes," she said with a shy smile. "But maybe it's time I do something different."

"Very well," he said with a shrug, leaning over to the other side and reaching into his bag. He held out a pair of white gloves, identical to those he wore. "Best put these on."

She took them from him, their fingers – though his glove-clad – brushing against one another as they did, sending a slight, not unwelcome shiver though her.

Hope slid on the gloves, and he shuffled the book left on the table so that it sat between them, returning it to the first page.

"Go page by page," he instructed. "You read the left side and I will read the right."

She nodded. "Very well."

They worked in silence for a time, with the viscount

asking her when she was ready for him to turn the page. She nodded each time, always slightly ahead of him.

"Do not go too fast," he instructed, and she tilted her head toward him with pursed lips, so that he was aware she was disgruntled at his tone. When she did, she noted how close his face was to hers. It looked different this close. She could see every whisker, every wrinkle, and even his grey eyes held a slight bit of warmth.

"I am not," she countered, and he raised a brow.

"I am a fast reader," she insisted. "But I am going one word at a time, I promise."

"Fine," he said, turning back to the page in front of them.

It wasn't until the twenty-fourth page that Hope found what they might be looking for.

"Here!" she exclaimed, and he turned quickly toward where she pointed, careful not to touch the page, even with the gloves. "The word *summer* again. It's underlined."

"You're right," he said. "But what does that tell us?"

Hope had no idea and wanted to tell him that *he* was the codebreaker, but she had a feeling he wouldn't be pleased with her if she did.

"There's a number in the heading on the page," he said, pointing at the top. "A year. 1457. I wonder…"

He wasn't speaking now, as he leaned over to look at the second book, and he quickly flipped it to page 14.

"Yes," he whispered triumphantly, and Hope shifted closer to him just as he was moving back to write on a piece of paper in front of him. Their shoulders collided, and Hope, caught off-guard, tilted to the left. Lord Whitehall reached out with quick reflexes and caught her before she slipped from the chair.

"Sorry," he mumbled, and she nodded, his hands warm where they rested on her arms now, as he hadn't yet removed them.

"Thank you," she said, hating the breathiness in her voice, and he released her so quickly that she nearly fell off her seat again. "What did you find?" she asked, recovering.

"I didn't find anything," he said, "but I have an idea on how this clue might be solved."

"And?"

"I'm on the fourteenth page of the second book. Now I just must determine if I choose the fifty-seventh word or letter..."

"Try the word," Hope suggested, and he nodded.

"I was going to start there."

He found the first word, "home," and wrote it on the paper.

"Now what?" she asked.

"Now we have to keep reading the first book until we find the word again," he said. "This is going to take some time."

"Good thing we have plenty of it," she said cheerily, and he eyed her critically.

"Are you always like this?"

"Like what?"

"So... *cheerful*." He said the word almost with disgust, and Hope leaned back away from him, not pleased with how much his criticism hurt.

"I cannot see what is wrong with that."

"Life isn't cheerful. Life is hard."

"So it is," she said carefully. "I would never deny that. But how dreary it would be to focus on those aspects of it. Yes, difficult things occur more often than we'd like, but isn't it better to enjoy the good parts?"

He let out a noise that was something like a harumph. "Until it comes crumbling down around you. And the higher you climb, the harder you fall."

Hope considered what he said for a moment, before

shaking her head vehemently. "I don't believe that's true. Pain comes either way."

"Believe what you'd like," he said, his eyes not leaving the book in front of him. "You've obviously never had anything untoward happen to you."

"That is not entirely true," she said, "although I have been fortunate, yes, I realize that. What happened that has caused you such pain?"

He finally looked up at her, his eyes focused and judging.

"You clearly do not understand, so I'm not going to waste my time speaking of it."

"You began this conversation," she said in exasperation, lifting her hands out to the side.

"So I did," he replied tersely. "But your father was right. You should never have come in here." He reached out and shut the book that was sitting open between them, moving it back to the other side. "You need to leave."

"This is my house. I can go where I please."

"Fine," he said, his teeth gritted. "I am *asking* you to leave. I work better alone."

"But—"

She could see only his side profile, and her breath caught. There was anger there, yes, but something more – pain. Pain that he did not want her to see.

"Very well," she said quietly, pulling the gloves off her hands and setting them down carefully on the desk. "Best of luck."

And with that she walked out, leaving him sulking behind her.

CHAPTER 7

*A*nthony knew he had been an ass. But he couldn't help it. There was something about Hope Newfield that got under his skin, that made him… feel things. And he didn't like feeling things. Not at all.

Which was why he considered that his best tactic was to do as her father had requested and keep as much distance between them as possible. Fortunately, she had avoided him for the rest of the day, until the dinner hour had arrived.

"I have the most wonderful idea," Lady Embury was saying now – of course, the only one talking.

"Oh?" Anthony's mother said, and even he had to admit that there was light in her eyes that he enjoyed seeing again.

"The market is open tomorrow in Harwich. Why do we not attend?"

"Oh, Mother," Lady Faith said in a disapproving tone. "I hardly think Lady Whitehall would enjoy herself there. It is simply people peddling their goods."

"Not just that, Faith," her mother said, raising a finger. "My maid tells me that tomorrow is a particularly *special* market day. There is a fair travelling through town."

"A fair."

"Yes." Lady Embury nodded emphatically. "They are bringing all kinds of exotic displays, as well as rides to partake in."

"What kind of rides?" Lady Hope asked, interest in her voice – which of course there would be. The woman was interested in everything, no matter how dull or ridiculous.

"Apparently there is a carousel, on which one can ride wooden horses. And even a sleigh that can be ridden down a hill!"

"That sounds fun," Lady Hope said with so much enthusiasm that Anthony had to keep himself from rolling his eyes. Did she really look forward to everything with so much joy? Was she not aware that would only lead to disappointment when it was not as "fun" as she thought it might be?

"Will you come, Sophia?" Lady Embury asked Anthony's mother, who nodded, her hands held tightly together in front of her.

"Of course. I would love it," his mother said, and Anthony sighed. That meant he would have to attend as well, taking a day away from breaking the code. He'd thought that he had figured out how to solve it, but so far, the words he had found based on his clue-breaking made no sense at all.

"I'm not sure about this," Lord Embury said firmly, biting into a thick piece of beef, and Lady Embury turned to him with a pout.

"It would only be for an afternoon, as Harwich is so close," she said. "Besides, it would be a wonderful way to show Sophia the countryside. Your lands have been so well kept," she said, smiling as she placed a hand on his sleeve. The earl's self-satisfied expression told Anthony that his wife was well aware how to convince him into doing whatever she pleased.

"Very well. One afternoon," he said, and his wife clapped her hands together.

"I'm so glad. You will come?"

"I'm not sure about that."

"Oh, but you must! We cannot go alone."

The earl wiped his mouth with an edge of the tablecloth. "Very well."

Hope beamed at her father, while even Faith didn't seem completely perturbed by the idea.

"We shall all leave at noon tomorrow," Lady Embury said. "Be prepared – for the most wonderful time!"

Oh, yes, Anthony would be prepared. Prepared to leave the fair as soon as he was able. Perhaps if he had his own horse, he could feign some kind of illness and leave early. Although he wouldn't want to leave his mother alone. He could only imagine the kind of people that would accompany a travelling fair, and he didn't want to think about what the "exotic" might mean. He supposed he would find out tomorrow.

He just had to get through an insufferable evening first.

* * *

"WHAT DO you think of the viscount?" Hope asked her sister as they prepared to leave for the fair the next morning. The truth was, she didn't much like the mention of the exotic, but the rides were intriguing, if not slightly frightening.

"He is a sullen man, thinks highly of himself, and is not much interested in the feelings or opinions of others," Faith said, walking over to her vanity and selecting a small necklace. She passed it to her maid, who fixed the clasp around her neck.

"Do you think so?" Hope said, trying not to show any

particular interest. "He seems so… hard. As though he has been hurt before."

"His family is the one who has hurt others. He has nothing to complain about."

"What do you mean?"

"His father was a traitor."

Hope's mouth opened in shock. This was the second time a member of her family had used that word regarding the viscount's father. "That cannot be true," she said once she regained her voice, shaking her head. "His mother is so kind, and *our* mother would never befriend the wife of a traitor."

"No, but she and Mother were childhood friends. Mother has been loyal to her, even after her husband defected."

"Do you know what happened?" Hope asked, and Faith shook her head.

"No. Father never shared with me the entire story. I only know that during the wars against the French he was a code-breaker and was later branded a traitor. Nothing could be proven so he was never brought to justice for his crimes, although he remained out of society until his passing. I believe it was quite difficult for Lady Embury."

"I'm surprised you do not know the full story," Hope said, perhaps a bit provocatively. "You usually discover all there is to know."

Faith tilted her head to look up at her. "I do not know *everything*."

"You seem to," Hope said, and Faith smiled as she shook her head and put on her pelisse. Hope took a breath, needing to ask her sister something that had been on her mind as of late. "Faith, do you truly not mean to find a husband?"

Faith's smile fell. "Why are you asking me of this again?"

"I just… I am saddened to think of you alone."

"I have you."

"Yes, but what if I marry?"

50

"Why this sudden talk of marriage?" Faith asked, placing her hands on her hips. "You do not have anyone in mind, do you?"

"No," Hope shook her head. "But we are getting to that age where it is expected of us, and I know Father is hoping that you marry first."

"Which makes no sense. I shouldn't hold you back," Faith said, lifting her hands in the air.

"Father is quite intent on it."

"He wouldn't say no if you found someone *appropriate*," she said, fixing Hope with a pointed look.

"I have no feelings toward the viscount, if that is what you are insinuating," Hope said. "Besides interest in what he is doing and appreciation that he is helping Cassandra's family."

"So you say," Faith said. "His is not a family that you want to tie yourself to. Remember that." She paused. "Besides, Father would never allow it."

Hope followed Faith out of the room on their way to meet the rest of their party at the carriages. "This is not an issue regarding which you need to have any concern."

"Good," Faith said, looking back over her shoulder. "Remember that."

Hope sighed as they reached the bottom of the stairs before going out into the fresh air beyond, where her father and Lord Whitehall were sitting upon their horses beside the carriage. This was perhaps going to be a long day – but she wouldn't dwell on that. Instead, she would think about everything of interest that awaited.

She was sure it would be much better than she thought.

* * *

THE RIDE into Harwich was a short one. Hope had refused to even meet Lord Whitehall's eyes after he had so rudely dismissed her yesterday. She understood that there was tragedy in his past that caused him to be the way he was, but that didn't excuse his rudeness.

She had only been trying to help, and he had reacted with malice for no reason whatsoever.

His mother was actually quite a sweet woman, if quiet and hesitant. Although that made her the perfect companion for Hope's mother.

"You were friends since you were girls, were you not?" Hope asked, to which her mother nodded. "Then why has it been so long since you two have seen one another?"

Lady Whitehall looked down at her lap while Hope's mother smiled brightly if slightly falsely. "We were both busy with our families. It has been fortunate we can spend time together once again."

"Of course," Lady Whitehall murmured.

Hope felt Faith's warning look upon her, but she ignored her.

"Well, I am happy to have the opportunity to become more familiar with you, Lady Whitehall," she said. "Especially as your estate is so close. Do you spend much time in the country?"

"I did until more recently," Lady Whitehall said. "Anthony prefers London, and I become rather lonely at the estate alone."

"All the more reason to prolong your visit here," Hope's mother interjected. "Now, what do you suppose will be at the fair? It has been such a long time since I have even been to the market, but a *fair*? What fun this will be."

Hope forced a smile of interest on her face as she allowed her mother to chatter on. It seemed she was not going to solve the mystery of Lord Whitehall – past or current. She knew she should let it go and do as her father and Faith said, keeping her distance from the viscount.

But, for once, she just couldn't seem to do as she was told.

* * *

THE RIDE into Harwich had been a silent one.

With the women filling the carriage, Anthony and Lord Embury had elected to ride beside the carriage, which Anthony was particularly pleased about, of course, although he wasn't about to confess his weakness to the earl.

Anthony was never one to strike up conversation at any time. He was not particularly inclined to do so with Lord Embury – not after the man had made it very clear that he had no wish for Anthony's presence in his home. Embury was obviously not particularly enthralled with the idea of him working with his precious book, even if he had only been holding onto it until someone had come along to break the code.

Anthony had a feeling that if it hadn't been for Hope, he would never have been given the opportunity to even look at it. He didn't appreciate having to leave the books behind at Newfield Manor, although the earl had locked them away back in the desk and had assured him that they would be safe, that no one else would solve the desk's code in the short time they were gone. Anthony wondered if he was, in his own way, giving him a compliment.

"How long do you suppose you will be staying at Newfield?" The earl asked him now, just as the town of Harwich came into view in front of them.

"My preference would be until I break the code," Anthony said. "But I suppose it will also depend on my mother's wishes."

"Your mother is not the same woman she once was," Lord

Embury said, surprising Anthony. He would have supposed that such a topic of conversation would not be of interest to the earl.

"She has been through much ridicule at the hands of society," Anthony said in clipped tones. "My father did all he could to shield her from it, but it is difficult to remain in good spirits when all of the *ton* speaks your name only in gossip and biting remarks."

"To be fair—"

"My father was not a traitor," Anthony said before the earl could get any words out. "I know you do not believe it, but someday, I will prove it. For my family name."

He waited for the earl to refute him, but instead the man only sighed heavily. "I hope for your mother's sake that you are correct," he said. "Lady Embury is a good woman, and she has always been a loyal friend to my wife. I understand that I have not been welcoming to you, but you must realize that I am doing so to protect my family. I have two daughters, both of marriageable age, and to have their names sullied could be disastrous for any prospects they might have."

Anthony was silent for a moment, knowing that this was the very reason no nobleman would ever have interest in marrying a daughter to him – not even if it was thought he had compromised her.

Which was why it was easier to stay well away from any chance of being denied. The situation with Lady Hope had been an unpreventable anomaly.

Still, he couldn't help the urge to prove himself – to this man and every other who no longer believed in the Davenport name nor the Whitehall title. He would show them all the man his father truly had been.

He just had to get through this blasted fair first.

CHAPTER 8

*T*his was madness.

Harwich had come into view at about the same time that the smell of the sea reached Anthony, beckoning him beyond. He actually would have enjoyed passing up the town altogether to look out over the harbour, but no, that was not their destination ~ instead, it was the monstrosity immediately before them.

On this side of Harwich, which Anthony guessed was normally a meadow grazing area, were now caravans and stalls and what he supposed were meant to be attractions of all sorts. If that wasn't enough to convince him to run in the other direction, it was the number of people who were walking between the stalls. The closer they came, the more he could see what awaited him. Smells of roasting meats and nuts, sugary and savory, blended together to overtake the salt of the sea, while spectators were ogling both the food before them as well as the people and animals sitting on stools and behind the bars of cages.

Anthony looked over to see Hope's head pop out of the

carriage window, one hand on the bonnet that covered her light hair.

"Goodness," he heard her say. "This is… something."

He supposed, for Lady Hope, that was a rather critical comment.

They drove the carriage and horses to an opening on the near side of the fair. Their driver and footmen would remain with the animals and vehicle to make sure they were looked after and no one would thieve them while they were otherwise distracted – and Anthony had a feeling that they were at great risk here at this type of event, which attracted all kinds.

He passed over the reins of his horse before stepping toward the carriage and lifting up a hand for his mother, whose eyes were wide as she walked down the stairs and took the awaiting fair.

"If this is too many people for you, I understand," he murmured, but she pressed her lips together and shook her head.

"It may be a lot of people, Anthony, but I don't know any of them," she said, the slightest of smiles lighting her face. "To them, I am just another face."

"Very well," he said, holding out an elbow for her, and the six of them began walking, the Newfield family in front of them.

Lady Embury kept turning her head to talk to his mother, and after the last "Sophia, do you see—" Lord Embury turned around to Anthony.

"Whitehall, why do we not let the ladies walk together?"

Anthony nodded as his mother joined Lady Embury up ahead. They walked in pairs in order to fit amongst the crowd, and Anthony soon found Lady Hope beside him.

She kept her head fixed straight in front of her, and he had the feeling that she was sore from their conversation the day before.

He cleared his throat as he clasped his hands behind his back. He didn't often apologize, but he also found himself strangely displeased with animosity between them.

"I apologize for my harshness yesterday," he said, his words stilted. "I did not wish to speak of the past, but I could have been more understanding in my wording."

She dipped her head for a moment, and he could almost see her thinking.

"Thank you," she finally said. "I suppose I am also at fault for trying to push you to speak of something you had no desire to address."

He nodded his own thanks, just before a rainbow bird began screeching at them from within a cage they were walking past. Hope jumped as it yelled "ahoy!" and Anthony reached out a hand, placing it on hers to calm her.

If she was anyone else, he would have allowed her to save herself – or waited for someone else to comfort her – but he couldn't help admitting that he kind of liked the way she felt beneath his touch.

"Would the lady like to hold the parrot?" a man asked, leaning out in front of them, and Anthony looked to Hope, who shook her head, so he growled "no" to the man before they continued on.

"I must confess something," Hope said, her voice soft as they passed a "bearded lady" who was quite obviously a man wearing a dress.

"Yes?"

"I do not particularly enjoy these kinds of displays," she said, her voice so soft it was nearly a whisper, as though she didn't want anyone to overhear her and be insulted. "It seems rather cruel, to leer at people or animals just because of the way they look."

"I agree with you," Anthony said, as it eerily reminded him of the way people used to stare at his family when they walked by, as though they were trying to determine just what traitors looked like. "Why do we not go find something to eat instead? It appears the market is on the other side of this fair."

She nodded her thanks, and when they asked her, Lady Faith agreed to accompany them.

"Roasted almonds, anyone?" he asked when he picked up the scent of cinnamon and sugar, and both women nodded their heads. He even bought some for himself, unable to resist the promise of sweetness, even though he knew it shouldn't be for him.

"Thank you," Lady Hope said with a smile, while Lady Faith still eyed him warily.

"Where to now?" he asked.

"I think I'd like to walk through the market, to perhaps buy some items from the local sellers," Lady Hope said.

"Very well," he said, but before they could start that way, Lady Faith was shaking her head.

"No," she said. "If we spend too much time there, then all will expect us to buy something from them. It will seem as though we have a preference for a select few."

"I do not think they would mind, Faith," Hope said gently. "Even a friendly word shows that we care."

But Lady Faith was still shaking her head. "Do not raise their expectations, Hope," she said. "It is best we return to the fair itself. Besides, Father and Mother will not want us to stray far."

Hope's disappointment was clear, but she nodded and began following after her sister. Anthony placed a hand gently on her arm.

"Why do you do that?"

"Do what?"

"Whatever she tells you to do."

"I—" Lady Hope blinked her eyes as she looked at him,

58

almost as though she hadn't realized what she had been doing. "It does not matter that much to me, whereas Faith seems quite convinced. If it will make Faith content to return to the fair, then I am happy to do it."

"You should think of yourself sometimes."

"Lord Whitehall, it is fine," she said, a smile on her face but her voice firm.

"It is not," he said, shaking his head.

"This is how things are between me and my sister," she said. "Now, we best follow her before we lose her in the crowd."

Anthony did allow her to lead him forward, but he didn't enjoy the turn of the conversation. This was what bothered him about Lady Hope – she never did as she pleased, always preferring to act in deference to everyone around her.

Although why that made any difference to him, he had no idea. He was only spending time with their family while he solved this code and then he would return home once more. Lady Hope was none of his concern.

And he would do very well to remember that.

HOPE HAD THOUGHT the fair would be a lot more entertaining than it was. So far, the food had been the only part of it that had truly interested her. The roasted almonds had been heavenly, and she wished she could have spent more time in the market. But it wasn't worth antagonizing Faith, which she wished that Lord Whitehall would understand.

Instead, they were now back to the fair, but she couldn't bring herself to walk through the exotic displays once more. Faith had rejoined their mother, and so Hope tugged on Lord Whitehall's sleeve, as she guessed he would be the only one willing to accompany her to where she wanted to go.

"The fair rides are over that way," she said. "Would you come with me?"

His gaze followed her finger to where the roundabout had been situated.

"Are you sure you'd like to partake?" he asked her. "I'm not sure I quite like the precarious look of it. How was it assembled so quickly? I doubt it is completely safe."

She laughed lightly.

"Why, Lord Whitehall, are you frightened?"

"Of course not."

"Then what is the harm? It is low to the ground and turned manually by a crank. It seems like it would be much fun."

His face twisted in a grimace that told her he thought it would be something quite other than *fun*, but she wasn't overly concerned. It would be good for him to have a little joy in his life, to allow himself some freedom to do things he wouldn't normally agree to.

He let out a sigh so quiet she almost didn't hear it before he led her toward the contraption. She did wonder how they had configured it so quickly, but surely, they must know what they were doing, did they not? It was not as though Harwich was the first town the fair had visited.

It was rather charming. A menagerie of wooden animals were attached to the arms that stretched out from the centre, and Hope skipped toward the ride, choosing a small wooden horse, sitting on it as though she was riding side-saddle.

"I am not sure you should be doing this," Lord Whitehall grunted, and Hope smiled at him.

"I'm certain it's fine," she said. "What harm could it do?"

He grunted out a "hmm" as he turned around, the only seat left for him the large lion in front of her, and Hope had to hold in her laughter as she watched how gingerly he climbed over top of it, his leg swinging around.

After a few more moments, a man called out a countdown, and with a groan, the entire apparatus began moving. Hope let out a slight squeal of glee, enjoying the rocking motion of the ride. It was only when Lord Whitehall turned to the side that she noticed he appeared rather green.

"Are you all right, my lord?" she called out, but he simply nodded curtly, refusing to turn around to look at her.

The creaking continued, until suddenly it became much noisier, and there was a massive groan in the wood before, suddenly and inexplicably, one of the arms began to crack.

Hope looked up, uncertain, opening her mouth to call out a warning, but it all happened so quickly that she had no time to react.

Lord Whitehall, however, was already moving, diving forward, lifting the small child in front of him off his horse and leaping to the side before the arm above them fell, right where the child had just been. The breaking of the wood disrupted the balance of the entire apparatus, and Hope was so busy watching what happened that she began to wobble as she slid off the side of her horse. She was running down away from her seat when she fell into Lord Whitehall's arms, and he pulled her away, half-leading, half-dragging her until there was a safe distance between them and the roundabout.

Hope clutched onto his arms, panting, before she was able to recover from all that had happened and look around them. She had no time to say anything, however, as a woman was running up to them, tears running down her face, the boy from the roundabout in her arms.

"Thank you," she said, sniffing. "Thank you so much. You saved my son."

The boy, who appeared to be around eight years old, nodded with maturity beyond his years.

"Thank you, my lord."

"Of course," Lord Whitehall said, his arms still around Hope.

"What is going on here?" They turned as one to discover Hope's father storming toward them, pushing through the crowd of people who had gathered around the accident. "Unhand my daughter."

"Father," Hope said, stretching her arm out. "Lord White-hall was only aiding me as I nearly fell from the roundabout. He saved this boy," she said, gesturing toward the mother and son beside them as the woman nodded frantically.

"It's true," the woman said as Lord Whitehall took a step backward away from Hope. "If it hadn't been for him, I would have lost my son."

"The roundabout arm collapsed," Hope exclaimed, turning to the viscount, still feeling the loss of his presence. "How did you act so quickly?"

"I had just jumped off, as I was... rather queasy," he admitted with a grimace. "But thank goodness, as because I was already on my feet, I was able to make it to the boy in time."

Hope couldn't help but beam at him, though her father did not seem particularly pleased.

"Just why would you be on a roundabout, and with the viscount no less?" her father asked, quirking up one of his thick eyebrows.

"It was my idea," Hope admitted. "The viscount was not particularly pleased about it, but I convinced him to accompany me."

"We will discuss this later," her father said, obviously not wanting an audience to the conversation he wished to have with her. "Perhaps it is time to go."

"First, we must eat something," her mother countered, waving a hand, obviously not overly concerned with all that had occurred, even as the fair workers were quickly trying to clean up the mess despite the chaos that had ensued around them.

Lord Whitehall had wandered off, speaking with one of the workers, and when he returned, he caught her eye.

"No one was injured," he said in a low voice, and Hope breathed a sigh of relief.

"Thank goodness," she said, even as she couldn't stop herself from staring at him. For here was a man who, despite always appearing so contrary, had put himself at risk to save a child he had never met before.

It was… confusing.

And it made her more interested in him than ever.

CHAPTER 9

*A*nthony frowned as he sat across from Hope at a table in the Harwich Inn.

Despite all of the food available in the market, Lord Embury did not like the idea of his family eating in the open air with all of the other fairgoers, and so instead he had paid for a private dining room in the local inn.

Anthony guessed that the fair food would have been far preferable, but it was not as though anyone had asked him.

It had taken some time for his heart to return to its normal rhythm after the near catastrophe at the roundabout. As soon as he had seen the results of the machine's obviously hasty construction, he had been wary, and it appeared he had been correct in his musings. Thank goodness no one had been injured. He was glad that he had been able to save the life of the boy, although as soon as he had set him in his mother's arms, he'd only had one focus – Hope. If anything had happened to her...

But he didn't want to think of that – nor why he would have been so devastated had the worst occurred. Instead, he told himself to focus on returning to Newfield Manor and the code that he was here to break.

He was beginning to wish he had never agreed to come here.

Thank goodness the meal was almost finished.

"Are we ready to depart now?" Lord Embury asked, apparently as eager as Anthony to return. It seemed there was something they finally agreed upon.

"I was hoping we could briefly stop by the stage," Lady Embury said. "I heard there is a puppet show taking place. Hopefully, one with Punch and Joan. I always find them *so* entertaining."

"I'm not sure..." Lord Embury began.

"I'd like to go," Faith chimed in, and Lord Embury brought his thumb and forefinger to his forehead.

"Very well," he said with a sigh. "To the stage we go."

Anthony had never been a fan of puppet shows – they were so juvenile, and the characters could have solved everything by simply speaking to one another rather than allowing the great misunderstandings that continued to occur.

But, again, no one had asked him.

Lady Hope's smile was large as she watched with her family, and Anthony found that he was unable to focus on the show. He far preferred watching Lady Hope and her varied expressions instead. He didn't think she would ever be able to hide what she was thinking, for her every emotion, from concern to humor to embarrassment for the puppets – that, Anthony felt – was written in the furrow of her brows or the glint in her eye.

Despite his initial misgivings, he was surprised when the play was over. They had avoided the crowd with their ability to pay for seats at the outskirts of the audience, which pleased him as it made it easier to depart without concern over losing his mother – or Lady Hope – in the crowd.

As he mounted his horse to return, however, he was reminded that he would have to spend the ride with Lord Embury – and Lord Embury alone – and braced himself for the warnings that were sure to come after the debacle at the roundabout, but he found himself pleasantly surprised once more.

"Thank you," Lord Embury said gruffly, and Anthony looked up at him with question.

"For what?"

"For saving my daughter. I know she was not in immediate danger, not like the boy, but... I appreciate what you did for her."

"Of course," Anthony murmured, keeping his gaze ahead. The truth, one that he didn't like himself, was that he was willing to do whatever it took to keep her safe. Even if she didn't seem particularly prepared to do so herself.

It wasn't his role, that was for certain. But somehow, he seemed to want it to be.

* * *

ANTHONY COULD TELL something was amiss the moment they turned into the drive of Newfield Manor. The butler must have seen them coming, for the doors were open, as would be expected, except, instead of staff prepared to help them disembark and prepare for the dinner ahead as well as additional hands to see to the horses and carriage, it was a fretting housekeeper with her hands in her apron, an equally displeased butler, and footmen with grim expressions that awaited them.

"My lord," the butler said, striding down the drive,

awaiting the earl as he threw his leg over the side of his horse and jumped to the ground. "I have some distressing news."

"What is it, Humphries?" Lord Embury said urgently.

"It appears that there was a thief in the house."

"A what?" Lord Embury practically shouted, those thick eyebrows coming into a low vee over his forehead. "What are you talking about? What was taken?"

"That is what is most strange," the butler said, "for it appears that nothing of note is missing. One of the maids went into clean your study and noticed that it appeared rather dishevelled. Books were scattered about, papers on your desk strewn around. We did not think you would have left it in such a state; however, we did not think much of it until we went into the library. Books were everywhere. We have tried to set everything back to rights as best we can, but from what I can tell, some books are missing from your study shelves."

"Which ones?" the earl thundered.

"I'm not entirely sure," the butler said, his expression appearing contrite. "I do not know their titles well enough, but there were certainly empty spaces upon the shelves."

"This is preposterous!" The earl exclaimed, as the rest of his family appeared from the carriage, concern on all of the ladies' faces. "Why would someone come into Newfield Manor? And how could it have happened with all of the servants about?"

"I suppose they took advantage of you being out, my lord," Humphries said. "I have questioned the staff, but no one saw anything."

Anthony exchanged a look with Lady Hope and Lady Faith. He knew exactly what the thief had been after, but he didn't feel at liberty to say, not in front of the staff as well as the mothers. The intruder had been after the book, but whether he had found it or not remained to be seen.

"Lord Embury, why do we not go look for ourselves?" he said with a meaningful gaze, and the earl caught it and nodded.

"Very well."

As they entered the house together, Anthony kept his voice low.

"Someone is looking for the book – or books."

"I gathered," the earl returned. "But who would even know of it?"

"I don't know," Anthony said, shaking his head. "Do you recall Lord Covington and Lady Cassandra telling us they thought someone was shooting at them as they searched for the clue? It leads me to wonder if someone else has discovered this treasure hunt."

"Or someone who already knows of it has ulterior motives."

Anthony looked at him in some surprise. "Only our friends are privy to it."

The earl lifted a brow. "How well do you know your friends?"

Anthony said nothing as they continued on to the study. He thought he knew them quite well, but then, did anyone ever know anyone else as well as he thought he did?

He supposed someone could have talked to another party as well, which would have sparked interest.

Somehow along the way to Harwich and back, it seemed that he and the earl had become... allies, if nothing else. He wasn't sure if it was due to his actions at the roundabout, or if it was because he had agreed to the earl's terms when it came to studying the books, but apparently the earl somewhat trusted him, whether he was pleased about it or not.

He followed Lord Embury into the study now, finding that the servants had put it mostly to rights, but even Anthony could tell that something was off. Lord Embury rushed to the desk and ran a hand down the side where the panel was hidden from which the book had emerged last time, though, of course, the desk didn't give away its secrets with simply a touch.

He grunted as he began to lower himself to his knees, but Anthony held out a hand. "Allow me," he said as he shifted underneath the desk, lying down beneath it before beginning to slide the panels into position.

"How did you know the code, anyway?" the earl asked, and Anthony grunted. "Hope."

The earl said nothing to that, as it was then that the panel slid open – showing both books waiting inside.

"Thank the Lord," the earl said with a whoosh of breath, and Anthony agreed with him. He could hardly imagine returning to Gideon, Cassandra and the rest of their friends with the news that their path forward had been blocked, that he hadn't been able to keep the books safe for the short time he was supposed to be in possession of them.

"Who could possibly have arrived, unnoticed, in the middle of the day?" the earl asked, leaning back against the doorframe with his arms crossed. "There are enough servants around the manor that surely someone would have seen a stranger appear."

"One would think," Anthony said. "But consider all of the comings and goings. Food deliveries, the post, merchants. It would be easy to enter disguised. Hell, someone could even pretend to be a servant and walk through the house practically unnoticed, could they not?"

"I suppose," the earl said with a heavy sigh.

"Have you any new staff?" Anthony asked, to which the earl raised his thick shoulders.

"If we do, I am not aware of it. I leave that up to the butler and housekeeper. My wife will advise if need be."

"Perhaps look into it," Anthony said. "In the meantime, we must be careful with the books."

"When you're not working on them, best leave them in the desk," the earl said. "You have leave to enter my study when you need. Be sure that you are not followed or watched."

"Of course." Anthony said succinctly.

"Dinner will be served soon. I'll return them to the desk now," the earl said. To return the books to the desk, all that was required was to replace them in the recessed opening and shut the panel tight. The only way to open it was through the panels beneath the desk.

It was quite intriguing, and Anthony hadn't taken the chance to properly notice it before. That seemed to be a pattern for him.

He turned to leave but stopped when the earl called him back.

"Whitehall."

"Yes?"

"I've trusted you with my book, my home, and my daughters. Do not disappoint me."

At those words, Anthony's heart hardened. For he knew exactly why the earl had said it. It was a lot to trust him with, considering what he believed about Anthony's father.

He turned and left without saying another word, but it was a stark reminder that he was not welcome here. He had no claim over Lady Hope, and he was best to do his work and then leave as quickly as possible.

To think he could do any different would only be fooling himself.

CHAPTER 10

$\mathcal{H}$ope hardly saw Lord Whitehall over the next week. He spent nearly all of his time with the books in the library, taking many meals in his rooms as he mulled over the code. The only time he took away from his work was usually at dinner, when he was nearly silent, speaking only when required and never looking in her direction.

Many times, she had paused outside the doors of the library, hesitating in the entrance, wondering if she should see if he was interested in her help or discussing what had caused him to completely close off to her – not that he had been overly open before.

But each time, she kept walking. She had no ties to Lord Whitehall besides those regarding this treasure hunt and their connection to Cassandra and Gideon. He had no reason to explain himself to her, and she knew from past experience that if she tried to push him, he would only turn into his usual surly self and make her feel worse.

If this is what he wanted, then so be it.

This morning when she walked by – as the library just

happened to be on her path to the breakfast room – she heard a heavy sigh, and this time, she peeked within to see if she could discover just what had him so vexed.

He was sitting at his writing desk in the corner, the books spread out in front of him, his hands in his thick, dark hair which today was uncharacteristically unruly.

"Damn it," he cried out, as he sat back away from the books and threw down his quill pen, which surprised her, for she'd have thought he would have been much more careful with the ink around the books.

"Lord Whitehall?" she called out before she thought better of it, stepping into the room.

"Lady Hope," he said, pushing his chair back and rising to his feet, running a hand over his hair in an apparent attempt to tame it.

When he said nothing more, Hope was suddenly frozen in awkwardness, unsure what to say or why she had thought this might be a good idea.

"I-I'm sorry," she said, wringing her hands together. "I heard your sigh from the hall, and I thought I would see what was amiss, or if I could perhaps do anything to help."

He shook his head. "It's this code. I thought I had understood it, but it appears that I am unable to break it as I thought I would be able to. I'm afraid that you will be unable to help. As would most people." He paused, his brows lifting as though a thought had occurred to him. "Except…"

"Except?" she prompted.

"My father learned his craft from another," he murmured, more to himself than to her, it seemed. "They were rather close in age and remained good friends, even after…everything. He might have an idea."

"Could you write to him?" Hope asked brightly, glad that she was able to help him come up with an idea.

"No, he'd have to see the books," Lord Whitehall said,

rubbing his chin. "I would have to take them to him. He lives about two days' journey from here and, from what I know, would have no interest in making the trip. He is something of a recluse."

Hope's excitement vanished with his words. "My father will never allow you to take the books from here. Not his, anyway."

"Likely not," Lord Whitehall said, before lifting his chin and clasping his hands behind his back. "But perhaps he doesn't need to know that I have them. I will think on it."

Hope knew she was being dismissed, but she stepped forward anyway. "I do not suppose I could help you today? Perhaps provide a fresh perspective?"

"Are you so well versed on codes, then?"

Hope took a breath, attempting to shield herself from his words, reminding herself that this was his way of keeping people at a distance, and it had nothing to do with her.

"I believe I provided some help the last time I attempted."

"You did," he acknowledged before he returned his gaze to the books and lifted his hands in the air. "I suppose it couldn't hurt."

"That's the spirit," she said cheerily. "I shall go breakfast quickly and return. Do not forget to eat yourself."

"Of course," he said. "I shall take a break in a while."

"Very well," Hope said, lightness in her step as she left the room, pleased that, at least, he hadn't been completely opposed to her offer. "I shall see you soon."

She hummed a tune to herself as she entered the breakfast room, where she found her family already sitting around the table.

"Good morning," she said cheerily, to which they responded in kind. "Where is Lady Whitehall this morning?"

"Still abed," her mother said. "She said she was tired and requested breakfast in her room."

"I hope she is well," Hope said as she filled her plate at the sideboard.

"I'm sure she is fine."

As Hope took her seat, Faith set her teacup down and looked at the rest of them expectantly.

"I have decided that I am going to pay Percy a visit."

"Lady Persephone?" her mother said. "Why?"

"You are having such a delightful time with your friend," Faith said, defensiveness in her tone. "I thought that I could see mine. She extended the invitation for any time during the summer."

"But Faith, how am I to accompany you when I have Lady Whitehall here as a guest?"

"You do not need to come."

"You cannot visit unchaperoned!"

"She is right. You cannot go alone," her father said. "Perhaps Hope can accompany you."

"Hope is not a chaperone," her mother said, staring at her husband in shock. "Why would you suggest such a thing?"

Lord Embury shrugged. "Faith is nearing five and twenty. It is not as though she is some young innocent."

"Victor!"

"Very well. She is innocent, but not young," he said, to which Faith snorted, thankfully not insulted. "She could be a chaperone herself."

"Hope does not need to accompany me," Faith said, and Hope nearly dropped her fork, so surprised by how much her dismissal stung.

"You do not want me to accompany you?" she asked, and Faith lowered her head as she mumbled the next words.

"It is not that I do not wish for your company, Hope. It is just that we do everything together. Perhaps it is time I do something by myself. I am sure one day soon you will be married and I will be alone, anyway, so I might as well get used to it."

"Faith," Hope said, her heart breaking as she saw the pain her sister tried to hide behind her strong mask. "That is not true. You will marry."

"What if I do not wish to?"

"You know I will always make sure you are well looked after," the earl said, patting Faith's hand, "but you must remember, Faith, that I do not have a son. It is why you should marry — in addition to the fact that Hope shouldn't have to wait much longer. If you choose not to marry, then someday, when I am gone, this will all go to your cousin, William. I would hope that he would take pity on you, but he will have his own family and you can never be certain."

"I understand," Faith said, purposefully folding her napkin in her lap. "And I will look after myself. But we do not need to discuss this now. All I am concerned with at the moment is arranging a visit to see Percy. I would not be gone long. Perhaps two weeks at most. I will take my lady's maid, of course."

"I will think on it," the earl said.

"I'd like to leave tomorrow."

"Tomorrow!"

"Yes. That will give me time to return before Cassandra and Lord Covington's wedding."

"Well, I suppose I must think on it much quicker, then."

"As will I," said Hope.

She did enjoy Percy's company, but Percy had always been closer friends to Faith. Hope had a feeling that if she accompanied Faith, she would be spending much of her time alone or tagging along behind the other two women, who would likely be happier without her.

She also wondered how much longer Lady Whitehall planned to be in residence – and just what her father would do if he discovered Lord Whitehall's plans to take the books away from Newfield Manor. She risked a glance at her father now, wondering if she should say anything. He was her family, after all, and her loyalty should be with him, but then, she didn't think that Lord Whitehall had any motive for taking the books besides solving the code.

How he would hide it from her father, she had no idea, but Lord Whitehall seemed to be a man who accomplished all that he put his mind to.

As she thought on it, a plan began to form in her mind. One that she knew could ruin her but, if she executed it perfectly, perhaps she could pull it off.

The worst consequence would be that she could be ruined, which would mean marriage to Lord Whitehall. And after all she had come to know about him, it couldn't be so bad… could it?

* * *

ANTHONY RISKED a quick glance at the library door. He had finally come up with a solution, one that he knew could be his undoing, but it was the only way he could see it forward.

He had to travel to see Reeves, his father's old friend, but he couldn't allow the earl to know that he would be taking the books.

He felt nearly sacrilegious doing what he was doing, but he knew it would work.

It had to.

He was just about to start when he sensed a presence in the room, and he swiftly lifted his head to find that Lady Hope had returned. Thank goodness he hadn't started.

"You didn't come for breakfast," she said, though her voice wasn't accusatory but rather questioning.

"I'm not hungry," he muttered, hoping to be rid of her quickly. "I have other things to attend to."

"I see," she said. "Have you decided what you are going to do?"

"Yes," he said. "I will depart tomorrow to see Reeves. I will take the books with me."

Hope bit her lip, and he could tell she was wondering whether or not she should trust him. He wished she would, but his hopes were soon dashed.

"I am coming with you," she said with confidence, to which he looked up at her and scoffed.

"You most certainly are not."

"I do not believe that is up to you."

"I believe it is," he countered. "I do not want an entire audience for this. If you come, then your mother comes. Part of the reason I am leaving is to get away from her incessant nattering."

"Lord Whitehall!"

"You know it is true," he said, which she couldn't deny.

"If your mother comes, then my mother comes. And everyone will want to know why we are going and what we are doing there. And then we return to the beginning of this conundrum, in which your father does not want the books to be removed from his residence. Besides, Reeves lives alone, outside the town, to escape people."

Her face remained impassive, and Anthony's cheeks heated as he realized he had said more than usual.

"I am not suggesting that I bring a chaperone."

He raised his brows. "You can hardly come alone."

"I have a plan so that no one will be the wiser."

"Lady Hope," he said slowly. "If you and I were to travel together alone, we would be required to marry."

"Am I really so bad?" she asked, obviously trying not to let him see how much his answer meant to her.

"It has nothing to do with you and everything to do with me," he said quietly. "Besides, your father told me to stay away from you while here in your residence. If he were ever to discover that you accompanied me on a journey away from the manor, I can hardly imagine how he might react."

"He would never know."

"I said no, Lady Hope. Now, if you'll excuse me, I have some preparations to make."

"I shall tell him what you are doing," she said, straightening her shoulders.

He snorted. "No, you won't. Good day, Lady Hope."

Clearly annoyed that he had seen through her ruse, Hope turned and left. Somehow Anthony had a feeling that this wasn't the last of this conversation. It was only the beginning.

CHAPTER 11

*A*fter all of Hope's insistence that she was secretly accompanying him on his journey, Anthony was surprised when, the next morning, he saw her standing at the door of the house, a valise in hand.

"What are you doing?" he asked, and she smiled sweetly.

"What I am doing has nothing to do with you," she said. "I am going with Faith to visit Lady Persephone."

"I see," he said, instantly dubious of her unsuspecting smile, but he wasn't sure what he had to be suspicious of. For there was Lady Faith, coming down the stairs, dressed in travelling clothes as well.

"Are you ready, Hope?" Lady Faith asked, and she nodded as Lord and Lady Embury, as well as Anthony's mother, entered the hall.

"I can hardly believe you are all leaving me at once!" Lady Embury said, clasping her hands together in front of her. "Although it shall not be for long."

"I suppose we will see you again in due time," Lord Embury said to Anthony.

"I am just going to consult with a friend and then I will be back to study the books," he said, keeping his gaze away from his valise, which held said books in it at the moment. "Thank you for looking after my mother."

"Of course," Lady Embury said with a warm smile, and Anthony was surprised that he actually felt something for the woman besides annoyance. Something akin to... gratitude? She did make his mother happy, and that was certainly worth something to him.

The ladies' carriage pulled up the drive, and Anthony hated the tug at his heart when he saw Lady Hope enter into it with a wave of her hand. This was for the best, he told himself. Hopefully, she wouldn't be here when he returned either, for then he wouldn't have to be tormented by her proximity once more. She was not for him, he continued to remind himself. It was about time he started acting upon that truth instead of just reminding himself of it.

The carriage started down the drive with dust rising behind it, and Anthony said his final farewells before walking down the gravel path toward the stables. He didn't feel like waiting around with Lord and Lady Embury any longer. He would walk himself to meet his carriage.

"My apologies for the wait, my lord," the stablemaster said when he arrived. "We are close to having your horses and carriage prepared."

"It's fine," he said, waving a hand. "The ladies are away now."

His driver and valet were already there, his valet storing his valise in the trunk of the carriage, and Anthony added his second – and much more important – small bag into the body of the carriage before he stepped out and waited in the sunshine of the day.

He closed his eyes and lifted his face. He could admit that days like this brought a touch of healing to his soul – even if it was only for brief periods of time.

Finally, the carriage emerged, and while Anthony wished he was riding, he knew that with the distance and the size of the books, it made the most sense to take the carriage. That way he could ensure that the books were safe, and it would give him additional time to study them.

He entered and sank into the plush blue interior, feeling every bit the entitled lord that he knew he was.

His family's reputation might be destroyed, but no one had ever proven his father a traitor, and therefore nothing had ever been taken away from them – except respect, and of course, his father himself. For he had died of a broken heart, as the country he had loved and risked his life for had turned its back on him.

Anthony sat in silence for a time, opening the window to allow the fresh air into the carriage. He found it helped keep his queasiness at bay. That was why he usually rode – when he was trapped inside the vehicle, his stomach did not appreciate the rocking back and forth. The one time he had travelled to the continent, he had sworn to himself he would never do so again, for the boat ride had nearly done him in. He had spent more time hanging over the railing than in his cabin.

He wasn't sure how long he had travelled – an hour at most – when he could have sworn something bumped against his foot. He started, looking around, wondering if a rodent had found its way into the carriage. He heard a scuffle and was instantly on alert, lifting his feet.

"Can you help me?"

"Bloody hell!" he yelled out, jumping from his seat and nearly falling over before he caught himself and realized it was the voice of a lady.

"I'm sorry."

Anthony was frozen in shock, hardly believing what he

was seeing as Lady Hope crawled out from beneath the seat he had been atop of just moments before.

"This is very untoward, I know, but it will all work out," she said as she sat herself down on the seat across from him, smoothing out her skirts and running a hand over her hair as though she was sitting on the sofa in the middle of the drawing room.

"Lady Hope," he finally said, rubbing his palms against his face as he tried to calm his rapidly beating heart. "Untoward is not the word. This is... this is..."

"I know," she said, a quite becoming pink blush rushing up her cheeks.

"How did you even fit underneath?"

"I am fairly small," she said, biting her lip. "My father would be livid if he found out I was here. And I know that you were not enamored with the idea of me accompanying you on this journey, but I swear, as long as your friend doesn't tell my father, we can keep this between us."

"And just how would we do that?" he asked, biting out the words.

"Well," she said, clasping her hands together. "Faith and I were on our way to Percy's, of course, and then I told Faith that I was actually feeling quite ill and would prefer to return home. So we did, and I disembarked with my valise. My maid – who can most certainly be trusted – helped me into your carriage in the stables while no one was looking. I told her that she could take the next week or two to visit with her beau. She was quite pleased about that. So my parents believe me to be with Faith, and Faith believes me to be with my parents."

She smiled prettily, but Anthony was already shaking his head.

"And what happens when Faith returns and they discuss the trip and Faith mentions that you were not there?"

"Oh, I will write to Faith when we arrive at our destination and tell her what happened. She will not be happy – not at all." She cringed at that. "But she will keep my secret. And I hope she will understand."

"Understand what?"

"That I *had* to accompany you. I never told Father about the books, but instead *I* will make sure that they are safe."

She seemed so proud of herself for apparently having everything figured out, but all Anthony could focus on was why she felt she had to do this.

"So you do not trust me."

"I never said that."

"Then why—"

"I am an extra set of eyes," she said in a rush. "What if you are called away for one reason or another? I can keep watch on them. We can work together."

"I'm going to tell my driver to turn around."

"No!" she said, raising a hand toward him desperately. "You cannot. If I return home, then what? I will be ruined for certain, for we could not keep it a secret any longer. Do you think your driver will keep my presence to himself? I hope he will, as he works for you and not my father."

Anthony sighed heavily as he sat back in his seat. It seemed she had thought of everything. Her plan was foolish, unnecessary, and actually rather insulting, but he didn't seem to have any choice but to follow along with it.

"I do not think this secret will be as easy to keep as you think it will be," he warned. "I can assure you that everyone who is faithful to me will not speak of it, but we will have to stop for the night, and who knows who we will see at the inn. Reeves never sees anyone, either. You should be more concerned about Faith's visit and what others might say to your parents. That, I have no control over."

"You are right," she said, her bottom lip coming between

her teeth. "We will likely have to include Percy in our plan as well."

He rolled his eyes. She was not understanding his point at all. But there was no way around it.

He was stuck with her.

* * *

Hope could practically feel the tension radiating off the viscount from his seat across from her. He was also sitting precariously close to the window, with his head almost hanging out of it like a dog.

"Are you all right?" she asked, leaning over to peer up at his face. "I know I surprised you, but—"

"Fine," he said curtly, his eyes still outside.

"Are you sure?" she said, inspecting him as best she could, moving so far forward that she nearly fell off the seat. "Because you don't look fine. You look... rather green."

"A bit queasy is all," he said, his words short. "I'll be better when we stop. Or if the road smooths out."

"It should, in a few miles hopefully," she said before a realization struck her. "That was why you were already off the roundabout when it broke. It made you feel sick."

"It did."

"Did you know it would, before you got on?"

"Yes."

"Then why—"

"You wanted to ride it. You said you would do so regardless of whether I did as well. So I got on."

"You should have told me."

He finally turned to her with exasperation.

"Would that have stopped you?"

"Yes."

"Well, it's a good thing we were there, or else the boy could have died."

"True," she said, mulling over the fact of how things often turned out the way they should. "Tell me about Reeves."

"Right now?"

"We are going to see him, are we not?" she asked. "I should know what to expect."

She was also hoping that distracting him would help with his queasiness.

"He and my father were good friends in their youth. Reeves was always fascinated with codes and was trained by his father. When additional codebreakers were required for the war effort, he recruited my father, as he had always been proficient at puzzles as well. They renewed their old friendship. Since my father died, however, Reeves has been a recluse. Do not expect him to be friendly or welcoming to you. Especially since he did not know that you would be accompanying me."

"But I will be arriving as your guest."

"Of a sort."

Hope decided to ignore that comment especially as he was, essentially, correct.

"Did he teach you, or did your father?"

"Mostly my father. But I spent some time with Reeves as well. He is brilliant and has studied nearly all of the codes that are known."

"I see," she said, biting her lip, wondering what was in store for her when they arrived. If Lord Whitehall, who was not exactly a polite conversationalist, was calling this man a rude recluse, she could hardly imagine how severe he might be.

"Is he married?"

"No, he never married."

"Is he part of the aristocracy?"

"Does it matter?"

"I was simply wondering." She kept the polite smile on her face, refraining from rolling her eyes. He always seemed to believe the worst about her, didn't he.

"A second son. His home is not grand but comfortable."

"I see."

"Will that be sufficient for you?" he asked, and she couldn't tell if his tone was cynical or teasing.

"Of course."

"How will you dress without a maid?"

"Allow me to worry about that," she said, even though this time, he actually had a valid concern. She had been thinking about it as well. She had tried to pack the gowns that would be easiest for her to fasten herself, but she had never had to do so before.

There was no better time than the present to learn.

And it seemed that there were going to be a lot of lessons in store for her. Perhaps the most pressing one? Patience.

CHAPTER 12

$\mathcal{A}$ nthony had tried to resist her questions. But by the time the carriage pulled up in front of the inn in Bures, they had been talking for nearly the entire carriage ride. Anthony could hardly believe it. He never entered into conversations like this – with anyone. He said what needed to be said and had no desire for the rest of it.

But somehow, with Lady Hope, it was different. Easier. She had asked about his upbringing, his schooling, about his friendships with the other gentlemen in his circle.

She'd asked him his favorite food, his favorite dance, what he did in his leisure time. Most of her questions, he'd never even considered before.

After a while, he had even asked her some in turn, which she had seemed happy to answer. It wasn't until they pulled up in front of the inn that he realized he hadn't thought of the arrangements for the night.

Apparently, judging by the look on her face, neither had she.

"Oh, dear," she said, as she took the hand he offered in

order to disembark. "I didn't realize that we would be stopping overnight."

"Foxearth cannot be made in a day," he said with a sigh. "Unless I had ridden." He couldn't help his pointed look toward her. "And then, I would never have had a stowaway."

"And your journey would not have been nearly as entertaining," she finished with a smile.

She was right about that, but he wasn't about to admit it.

"How shall this work?" she asked in a whisper, her arm curling around his as they walked slowly toward the entrance. The light had dimmed for the day, but the inn was alive. The attached tavern – one which he could certainly not take her to – was full, with guests still arriving. "I have no chaperone and no maid. I could pretend I am a widow, I suppose. But then how would we explain my relationship with you?"

"I suppose I could be your paramour."

His jest was worth the shocked look on her face, and he couldn't resist a small smile.

Her eyes narrowed when she realized that he had been teasing her, and she then brought her other index finger to her lips. "Perhaps I enter alone, pretending that I am an actress, on my way to join a theatre group. That would be most thrilling. What do you think?"

"I think that if others hear of an actress in a building – alone – who looks as you do, then you might attract attention of a kind that you would rather not receive. Besides," he looked her up and down. "You are not dressed the part."

"Isn't that the beauty of an actress – that I can be whoever I want?"

"Yes, but an actress would not be able to afford the clothing you are wearing. And I'm sure they will have already noticed that we arrived together. The servants will talk."

"I could be your sister," she said. "It is not nearly as exciting, but it would work."

The thought of her posing as his sister was most unwelcome, which didn't make a great deal of sense, but he also knew it would never be believable. A woman of her quality would most certainly have a chaperone, or barring that, a maid. But the truth was, no matter who she posed as, he could never allow her to stay in a room alone. Word travelled fast of single women in an inn, especially one as beautiful as she. He wouldn't be able to sleep all night for fear of what dangers might await her.

He stole a glance at her. The problem was, she was such an innocent that she would likely not even realize just *why* it would be too dangerous.

"It is not safe for you to stay alone," he said, and when she turned to him and opened her mouth, he held up a hand. "You chose to come along," he said, "and, unfortunately, there are some consequences. One being that a woman such as yourself would be too... tempting for men who might know of your whereabouts tonight."

"So what am I to do?" she asked with some dismay.

"You will have to pose as my wife. It is the only way to keep you safe."

She blinked at him. "Your *wife?*"

The sound of that should fill him with horror. And yet, somehow, it sounded rather... right.

"Yes," he grunted, not trusting himself to say more. "We will have to stay together, but of course I will see to your modesty."

"Very well," she said demurely, looking down and away from him as they stepped through the door into the inn, and he thought he could see her cheeks blushing a very deep pink. Well, then, it seemed he had some effect on her.

No one questioned them when they asked for a room, not

blinking when Anthony requested dinner to be received there. He took a moment to speak to his driver, explaining the situation as best he could, hoping he could trust the man with their secret, even if he wouldn't trust him around Lady Hope.

He didn't think he could trust *any* other man to look after her or keep her safe. It was a task that he seemed to have taken on himself, no matter how unwelcome it had originally seemed. He vowed to live up to that task – until this was finished, at least. For even though he knew her father would have his hide for allowing this to happen if he discovered them, at least he could assure him that he had done all in his power to return her as she had left.

"Well, then," Lady Hope said, turning about the room, her hands clasped in front of her, the smile on her face rather forced. "This is…"

Anthony smirked as he could tell she was searching for a word to positively describe their surroundings, but he wasn't sure that even she with her sunny light on everything she came into contact with would be able to come up with one for a room like this. He waited patiently, arms folded over his chest.

"Interesting," she finished.

"Interesting?" he repeated, hiding his smile. "And just what, pray tell, is interesting about it?"

"Well, the colors," she said, her eyes roving around the room. "The brown in the curtains and on the bed would hide any dirt. That is some ingenuity."

He laughed then. A deep laugh, one that came from his stomach, and she looked at him with so much surprise that he laughed even harder.

"I didn't think you could do it," he said.

"Do what?"

"Come up with a way to describe the hideousness of this room in a way that wasn't insulting."

"Well, it has obviously been well used over the years, hasn't it," she said.

"It most certainly has," he returned. "This is their best room."

She turned shocked eyes on him. "Their best."

"Yes," he said with another laugh. "It is."

He walked over to the bed and pulled back the blankets, taking a cursory look over the sheet beneath.

"From what I can tell, however, it is clean."

"That is comforting, I suppose."

A knock at the door signified the arrival of their food, and Anthony took it from the maid and set it out on the table in front of them.

"I can do that," Hope said, stepping toward him, but he shook his head as he carried the tray, their shoulders brushing against one another in the cramped space between the door and the table. Tingles ran through his body from where she had touched him, down his spine and straight to his core.

He paused for a moment, shocked by how the innocent touch of a woman could cause such a strong reaction within him, but he tried to shake it off before she noticed.

It was, however, too late.

"Is something amiss?"

"No," he said, more harshly than he meant to, but he was trying to deny what he was feeling. He set the tray down on the table, and she took a seat in the rickety wooden chair. He helped push her in closer, unable to take his eyes off her hands as she slowly removed her gloves – one finger at a time – before setting them down beside her.

The way she slid them off had him thinking of other ways

he could undress her – ways that he had no business thinking about.

He cleared his throat as he took a seat across from her, and it was only then that he actually saw what filled his plate.

"What do you suppose this is?" he asked, watching the way her nose crinkled as she stared down at the white and brown mashed up food before them.

"Well," she said, clearly attempting diplomacy, and when she swallowed, he noticed the bob in the long column of her throat. "I would say with certainty that there are potatoes somewhere on the plate, and some kind of meat. I suppose we won't know what it is until we try it. Perhaps peas some-where within? And of course, gravy overtop."

"Shall we find out?"

"I do not suppose we have much choice, unless we would like to go hungry."

"Which would never do."

"Very well, then," she said, taking a deep breath before picking up her fork and diving into her plate.

Anthony watched her take the first bite and waited to see how she would react.

Her eyes met his, and the side of her mouth quirked upward as she chewed.

"Coward," she said when she finished, and he snorted in response.

"Excuse me?"

"You are acting a coward!" she said indignantly. "You waited to try it yourself until you saw what I thought of it."

"And?"

"And I am not going to give you the satisfaction of any knowledge," she said, lifting her nose in the air.

"Lady Hope."

She waved her fork at him. "At this point, you might as

well just call me Hope, as it seems we will be spending a great deal of time together."

"Are you certain?"

She shrugged. "In private, anyway."

"Very well," he said, pausing, knowing what she expected but finding the familiarity uncomfortable, likely because he hadn't offered it to many. "Anthony... is fine for me."

"Oh, good," she said with a smile. When she took another bite, he figured that he must be safe to try some as well.

He hesitantly placed some of the food into his mouth and chewed slowly.

"This is oddly... not horrible."

She smiled widely. "Are you not glad I allowed you to discover that for yourself? Fortunate surprises can be such fun."

"I am not one for surprises."

"Not even good ones?" she asked.

"Not even those." He shook his head.

"Well, perhaps I can teach you to change your mind."

"I doubt it."

"We shall see."

They shared a small smile before returning to their food, and even though silence stretched between them, it was not uncomfortable. Not at all. In fact, for once, it felt rather... right. Again. And that bothered him more than he would like to admit.

For he already knew that he could not have this woman. Even if her father had not warned him off, he would never allow it himself. It was far too likely to end in disappointment, and he'd had enough disappointment for one lifetime.

CHAPTER 13

$\mathcal{H}$ope had actually grown quite comfortable around Anthony – until their shoulders had brushed and an odd tension had electrified the air.

It startled her, and she'd have felt foolish about it, except that she could see it had affected him as well. Luckily, the strange air between them had loosened somewhat once they had sat down to dinner, especially with his teasing banter, but now that they had finished, she couldn't help but continue to look over at the bed, which took up the majority of the room, as well as her thoughts.

Anthony followed her gaze, lids heavy over his grey eyes, although Hope couldn't quite read the expression within them.

"Do not be concerned about sleeping arrangements," he said. "I will leave the room while you prepare for bed and I will sleep on the floor."

"The floor?" she said, startled. "You cannot sleep on the floor."

"Well, I certainly cannot sleep on the bed with you."

"Why do you not tell the innkeepers that I have a maid

sleeping with me and ask for another bed to be brought in?" she asked as brightly as she could in order to hide her nerves.

"They saw us come in without a maid," he said, running a hand through his hair, and for the first time since she had stowed away in his carriage, Hope felt a tinge of regret at what she had done. She had obviously added a great deal of trouble to what was already a rather trying situation for him. "However," he mused, looking to the side, "I suppose a large number of husbands and wives sleep separately. I shall go speak with the innkeeper."

"Thank you," she said, relief rushing through her. She knew he could never sleep in the bed with her, but she didn't like the thought of him sleeping on the hard floor either.

"I'll take the tray," he murmured, gathering everything up, and she helped him as best she could. As she held the door for him to depart, she watched his back retreat down the stairs and considered that not many men in his position would be open to carrying trays, serving meals, and seeing to such menial tasks. But she supposed that was her fault, for he would not be hiding in the room if it wasn't for her.

Hope sank down onto the bed, her hands coming to her temples. Goodness, what had she done? This was likely the most reckless action she had ever taken in her life. She had thought it had been for a good cause. She had wanted to trust him, but hadn't been able to stop wondering what would happen if he left and they never saw the books again. Her father would not only be devastated, but he would blame her and Faith, for they had vouched for the viscount. If it wasn't for her, neither the viscount nor his mother would even have come to Newfield. So she had thought she would come along with him — only now she was feeling like quite the little idiot. If anyone ever found out about this, it would change her entire life – as well as Anthony's.

Anthony. She could tell that it had been difficult for him

to be so familiar with her, and she wondered if it was because he didn't want to give her the wrong impression, or if it was because he had never been so close to anyone before.

She would likely never know.

Hope was so immersed in her thoughts that she jumped when the door opened, and she brought a hand to her chest when she saw that it was Anthony returning.

"Are they coming to prepare the bed?" she asked, wringing her hands in worry when she noted he was frowning, his brows drawn low over his eyes.

"No. It's a busy night, being a popular destination as well as a busy time of year with the weather so favorable. They don't have any additional bedding, beds, or rooms. They told me we were lucky to get what we have."

"Oh, no," she said, her stomach dropping. "Well…"

"It's fine," he said. "I shall be out in the hall while you prepare for bed. Call when I may re-enter."

"Very well," she said, out of ideas, though the guilt was weighing heavily upon her. "Might I ask a favor before you go?"

"Yes."

"Could you please unfasten the back of my gown? I may have thought ahead in terms of what to pack, but I never considered the gown I was currently wearing."

She saw him swallow then nod, and she turned around to face the window of the room, which was so dirty she didn't think anyone could see in or out, before placing her hands on the bodice of the dress so that it wouldn't fall when the fastenings were loosened.

The tension between them was thick as he stepped toward her, and she braced herself in anticipation when he approached her back.

His breath was soft and warm upon her neck as his fingers

grazed over her shoulders while he loosened the first fastening. Her maid usually made quick work of them, but Anthony moved much slower and more methodically as he continued down her back. Every time he reached the next button, Hope had to focus on stilling her body so that she wouldn't shiver in anticipation of the stroke of his fingertips against her skin.

Finally, he reached the bottom, and the fabric of her dress parted at the back. She was sure he had a good look at the skin above her chemise, especially when it took a few moments for him to step back and away from her.

"I'll, ah…" He cleared his throat, "…be waiting outside."

And with that, he took off toward the door as though he was being chased by a wild boar.

She would have laughed if she wasn't so affected by their exchange.

Hope made quick work of removing the rest of her clothing, leaving her chemise on before adding her nightgown overtop. She considered her wrapper as well but decided that she would feel as though she was being suffocated if she wore it to sleep.

She dove under the covers before calling out, "come in," and when Anthony stepped through the door, her cheeks warmed as she wondered if he had heard her moving about. Most likely.

He said nothing as she faced the wall, the covers pulled up close to her shoulders. She never had much issue in making conversation – until now. But this was hardly a typical situation, so it made sense that awkwardness would ensue. Awkwardness… and awareness. She couldn't see him but could track him moving about the room. She squeezed her eyes tight and told herself not to look, but she couldn't resist shifting slightly to see what he was doing – and then she wished she hadn't. For he was down to his trousers and shirtsleeves, folding his cloak out over the floor in a makeshift bed.

"Take a pillow," she called out, her voice sounding too loud and shrill in the silence. She cleared her throat. "And anything else you might need."

"If you're not using it," he said, his voice lower and huskier, and he came over and took the one she held out to him. His cravat was gone, the top buttons of his shirt undone so that she could see the skin of his chest below, covered in a light patterning of hair. "Thank you."

Their eyes locked, and for a moment, Hope forgot to breathe, but then he stepped back and away from her, toward the fire. He lay down, settling in, and while he was the one on the floor, Hope wondered how she was ever going to get any sleep tonight.

* * *

ANTHONY KNEW he wasn't going to sleep a wink.

Of course, the hard floor was not exactly ideal, as he continued to shift to try to find some semblance of comfort. But whenever he did, another floorboard bit into his body and he found his arms going numb.

That wasn't the worst of it, however.

No, the worst of it was hearing Hope move around in the bed beyond. He wished that she would stop moving, but to ask her to do so would only make him look like an even bigger lout than he already was.

"Are you all right?" he finally asked, and as soon as he spoke, her rustling stopped.

"Fine," she said quickly, and he sighed before pushing himself up and walking over to the chair in the corner.

It had some padding on it still, though it was worn in most spots. He had dismissed it earlier, but he didn't think that anything could be worse than the floor had been.

He shifted, trying to find somewhere to rest his head, and that was when Hope sat up in bed, dimly visible by the light from the fire.

"This is ridiculous. You are never going to sleep like that," she said.

"I can sleep in the carriage tomorrow. Why are you not sleeping?"

"I cannot sleep knowing how uncomfortable you are."

"There is no point in both of us staying awake all night."

They both paused for a moment, before she responded, her voice hesitant. "Why do you not sleep on the other side of the bed? There is plenty of room. You can stay on top of the blankets."

"I couldn't do that."

"Why not?"

Because he would be too tempted to reach over and run a hand down the smooth skin of her arm, to lean in and see what she smelled like up close. He had been teased by her fresh, sweet scent before, and he longed for more of it.

"Because... you are an innocent young woman, and it wouldn't be right."

"Well, it isn't right for us to be sleeping in the same room together – alone – according to the rules of society, so I'm not sure what the difference would be in you at least getting a good night's sleep as well."

Little did she know that being close to her was the very reason he wouldn't sleep.

But even if sleep alluded him, the thought of having a bed to lie on instead of the floor or this equally uncomfortable chair was nearly as tempting as she was.

"Very well," he said, easing himself out of the chair and walking over to the bed. She scooted over until she was nearly falling off the other side, and so he did his part and stayed close to the edge away from her.

"Thank you," he said gruffly.

"Of course."

He listened to her breathing, knowing she wasn't sleeping either, but he was unsure how to ease this strain between them.

"Why is this so important to you?" he asked, surprising himself with the question.

"Sleeping?"

"No. The books. This journey."

She turned over, and he could tell she was now facing him, although he didn't quite trust himself to turn around and look her in the eye.

"I know how much this means to Cassandra, as well as to Gideon. I am happy to do what I can to help. And, to be honest... I have always felt that my life has lacked purpose, if that makes sense. All I do is sit around with my mother and sister, visiting other women and playing music for them. If I can help with this, then it would feel as though I am making a difference."

"Your music makes people happy."

"That's very kind of you, and I do enjoy it as well. But this is the opportunity to do something else. Something different. Something... good."

"And yet you didn't trust me to help you?"

"It is not that I didn't trust you," she said slowly. "I know that you would never do anything to jeopardize this mission. It's that I can help you make sure the books stay safe. I am concerned about what would happen if my father discovered that they were gone."

"He shouldn't."

"Why do you sound so confident?"

He turned over and faced her, seeing the openness on her

face in the dim light, realizing that he was seeing a rare side of her – one that was open with her concern, that didn't hide behind the smile she wore almost like a mask.

"Because I made it appear as though the book is still there," he said.

"How?"

"I switched out the pages. It was painstaking work, and if the books were worth anything, I have likely ruined them, but at least I know that your father won't come chasing after me. Us."

Her lips parted as she raised her brows. "That is ingenious."

"Most people would call it duplicitous."

"You had good intentions."

"I do."

"What do we do now?" she asked, her voice a whisper.

"Now?" he said. "We sleep."

CHAPTER 14

*W*hen light hit her eyelids, Hope raised her arms above her and to the side, stretching to greet the day – and then froze when her right hand collided with something solid. Something... *warm* and solid.

Anthony.

Just as she was about to sit up and scoot away from him, his arm reached around her, settling heavily overtop of her, and he pulled her in and up toward his body, his chest hard and warm against her back.

Hope's breath caught as she stilled. Was Anthony still sleeping? He must be. For not only did she know he would never allow himself such contact with her if he was awake, she was also aware that sleep had eluded him long into the night, as he had laid there rigidly beside her. It seemed cruel to wake him from his slumber now that he had found it, even though she knew he would want to get on the road soon.

And also, it felt... nice. Warm. Comforting, to lie in his embrace. She was sure he would be horrified with himself if he knew what he was doing, but maybe, for these few moments... she would simply enjoy it.

His hand was resting against the bare skin of her wrist beneath her nightgown sleeve, and he began to absently stroke her, his thumb making small circles. It was the lightest movement, soft and smooth, but it had her entire body on edge, making her feel warm and... tingly.

His body was wrapped around her from behind, and she couldn't help but nestle her bottom in closer against him, enjoying this rare show of affection – and then she felt something hard and straight nudge against her back.

Was he... no, but he couldn't be... well, maybe he was.

Hope might be innocent when it came to experience, but Cassandra had shared stories with them, and coupled with some of the books they so scandalously and secretly read in their book club, she knew more than most young women of the relations that occurred between men and women.

But Anthony didn't feel any affection or desire for her – did he?

"Hope," he murmured, his hand moving higher on her body, until it brushed against her breast, her body's reaction shocking her, the neediness rushing over her as she tried not to move against him for more. His head dipped, his lips nuzzling against her neck, and she couldn't help but lean into his touch, arching her neck to provide him with better access.

She had no idea if he was awake or asleep anymore, but at this moment, she no longer particularly cared. Even if he *was* sleeping, it was her name on his lips, meaning he was not as unaffected by her as he let on.

But she had to know – was he doing this because he was dreaming, or was he purposefully seducing her?

She wasn't entirely sure how she would react if he was.

Hope turned in his arms, causing his hand to splay across her back as she held her body just slightly away from him, knowing that if she pressed into him, this could go further than she bargained for.

His eyes were closed, but he was moving, his lips toward hers, seeking her out – and she thought she just might let him find her.

* * *

ANTHONY WAS HAVING the most wonderful dream.

Typically, the only vivid imaginings he had were nightmares he'd prefer to forget. But tonight... tonight he was dreaming of a beautiful blond woman in his arms, one who was soft in all the right places, who was innocent yet far too willing. Who made him forget all the reasons he wasn't going to allow himself to be with a woman, especially one who would expect not only commitment, but even worse – love. Affection.

In his dreams, however, he didn't have to worry about that. He could hold her tight, caress her, run his hand over the softness of her breast. He ran his lips over the long expanse of her neck, feeling her pulse beat rapidly beneath his touch. And then, when she turned to face him... that was when he crashed his lips down upon hers.

He drank her up, tasting her plush softness. She was hesitant at first, but the more he coaxed her with his touch, the bolder she became, until she was as much of an aggressor as he. And oh, he had never been so affected before, had never had a woman, especially one like her, so sweet and so loving, in his arms, giving what he knew she had never before offered another man.

He ran his hands up her arms, over her back, exploring her, seeking out her smooth skin. She was warm, pliant, comfortable in his touch.

When his tongue caressed the seam of her mouth, she

opened to him, and he was soon exploring her, showing her what it would be like if he were to take this further, to find the depths of the passion together.

And then she moaned, arching into him – and his eyes flew open with a start.

For this was no dream. Lady Hope Newfield was in his arms, her face tilted up toward his, her lips still accepting his kiss as her eyes remained closed.

Until, at his refusal to return to her, they slowly opened, blinking up at him, the blue within having taken on a watery, dreamlike quality.

"Anthony?" she whispered, and he forced himself to push up and away from her, leaning back against the old, scarred wooden headboard.

"Hope," he said, hearing the raspiness of his tone and clearing his throat. "Hope, my God, I am sorry. I didn't… that is, I—"

"You were asleep," she finished, dipping her head, disappointment in her tone.

"No, that is, I— well, yes. I thought I was dreaming."

"Of course," she said, pushing back herself until she was at the edge of the bed. "I shouldn't—we shouldn't have—"

"No," he said, taking a breath as he ran his hands through his hair. "At least we stopped."

"Yes, how fortunate," she said, surprising him with the sarcasm in her tone.

"Hope, I have compromised you as it is," he said, his tone harsher than he meant for it to be. "However, anything more would have truly ruined you. You do know that – don't you?"

"Think nothing of it," she said brightly, her demeanor changing in an instant. Anthony sighed, wishing she would show him what she was truly feeling, would say why she was upset instead of masking it. "We should get going, should we not?"

"I suppose so," he said, considering that he could always talk to her in the carriage. There would be plenty of time in their forced proximity. He stood, annoyed to find that his hands were shaking slightly as he began to button his shirt, then sought out his waistcoat and jacket. "I shall go find us something to eat while you prepare yourself for the day. Coffee or tea?"

"P-pardon?" she said, turning her neck to look at him.

"Do you prefer coffee or tea?" he repeated, wondering if she hated him for what he had done. He wanted to ask, but he didn't want to upset her any further. They were in somewhat of an impossible situation, as he was sure she would now want to return home, but he would lose two days of time if they did so.

"Tea."

"Of course," he said before letting himself out the door, leaning back against it after it closed and taking a deep breath.

He had nearly lost all sense of reason and inhibition with Hope. She would likely now expect marriage, as would Lord Newfield if he ever learned about this – that was, if he didn't first kill Anthony.

One thing was for certain. Wherever they next stayed, they were going to come up with a better cover story. He could not subject himself to such temptation once more. For if she responded to him as she had again, he wasn't sure that he would be able to stop himself next time.

* * *

HOPE PRESSED her knees tightly together, her palms between them as she and Anthony sat on opposite carriage seats in silence.

She kept stealing glances at him, but his gaze remained

fixed out the window, either because he didn't want to look at her or because he was trying to prevent his queasiness.

She also wasn't sure which answer she would prefer.

"How long until we arrive?" she finally asked, breaking the silence.

"A couple of hours."

"I see. Is Reeves expecting us then?"

"He is expecting me."

"Right."

While she had broken him into discussion yesterday, it seemed that now she had to start from the beginning once more. She sighed as she wondered whether she had it in her to do so again, but she hated this unspoken conflict between them and wished to find ease. She decided there was only one to go about it, and that was to be direct with him.

She took a deep breath for courage.

"Anthony, perhaps we should discuss what occurred this morning."

"I sincerely apologize for that," he said, his jaw tightening slightly. "It was a mistake. A mistake that began when I joined you on the bed. It will not happen again." His eyes flickered over to her face. "I realize what this means and if you expect me to do right by you… I will."

Hope's eyes widened. "Anthony, I did not accompany you on this journey to trap you into marriage."

"I know, but—"

"I am aware that this is my fault, and I will not hold you accountable. I was the one who stowed away in your carriage, even when you told me not to come on this trip. I was the one who brought no maid and therefore could not stay in my own room. And I was the one who told you to join me in the bed. You took… actions in your sleep that I cannot fault you for, although I do have to ask—"

No. She shouldn't. She shouldn't ask.

"Ask what?"

"Nothing."

"Say it," he said, his eyes trained on her, and she opened her mouth with some trepidation.

Her voice just above a whisper, she asked, "Did you want a woman, or did you want... me?"

He stared at her, his nostrils flaring slightly, his eyes narrowing. "What do you think?"

"Well," she said slowly. "At first I thought you considered me just a woman in your bed, but then you said my name."

He didn't respond, and she did her best to be patient, to not fill the silence but allow him to speak.

"I had just spent the day with you, Hope, and you are a beautiful woman," he finally said. "Make of that what you will."

It appeared that was all she was going to get from him, as he lapsed back into silence and stared out the window.

It wasn't his response that Hope couldn't stop thinking about. It was the fact that, even though she knew he likely only wanted her for her availability, he did not appear to actually like anything about her. He was the one man her father – and Faith – had forbid she consider as anything more than an acquaintance.

Yet she couldn't help but want him to kiss her again.

CHAPTER 15

*A*s the small country cottage came into view from the carriage window, Anthony breathed a sigh of relief. For not only was he glad that their journey was over – and his rocking stomach could be set at ease – but arriving at Tom Reeves' residence also felt like a coming home for him. He had spent many days here, at the side of his father, and he figured it was the closest he would ever come to feeling like he was with him once more.

He stole a glance at Hope. Not that this was something he was going to share with her. She had learned far too much about him already.

Anthony exited the carriage quietly and stretched out his arm as an invitation for her to join him. She took it, and for a moment, a flash of emotion at how right it felt to be arriving together ran through him, but he quickly dismissed it. She had stowed away, he reminded himself. She had no business being here at all, and there was still a very real chance that they could be discovered and their fates become forever entwined.

Reeves' tall figure filled the doorway of the cottage. His

hair was greyer than the last time Anthony had seen him, and his reluctant smile faltered somewhat when he saw that Anthony wasn't alone. He had never been a particularly social man, but since the accusations that had been thrown at Anthony's father, he had practically turned into a recluse.

The cottage had aged like the man, the wood worn and the thatched roof showing its years, but the grey stone and cobbled walls were as solid as ever.

"Anthony. Good to see you, my boy," Reeves said when they neared, his eyes darting over to Hope. "I see you have company. Are congratulations in order?"

"Mr. Reeves," Hope greeted him softly, lowering her head.

"This is Lady Hope," Anthony said. "She is a… friend of mine."

"I see," Reeves said, not asking the further questions that most people would. He stared at Hope for a long, solemn moment, and then gestured them forward.

"Come inside," he said, and ducked back through the door and into the cottage, Hope and Anthony following.

The large sitting room made up the majority of the cottage, with the small cookstove and table to the side. It was not as sparsely decorated as one might think upon meeting Reeves. Instead, it was covered with quilted prints and paintings that Anthony knew had been created by Reeves' mother years ago.

Bookshelves lined the walls, filled with a mixture of fiction, history, and books about riddles and codes that had fascinated Reeves all his life. The crackling fire in the stone hearth cast its warm light on the dark wood panelling of the walls.

"I was surprised to hear from you, Anthony," Reeves said, taking a well-worn upholstered chair and gesturing toward a sun-faded sofa, its once vibrant colors muted by time, for Anthony and Hope to sit upon. "I would never have guessed that you would be interested in continuing on in the profession after all that happened to your father."

He was right. Anthony had never expected to do this again.

"This is a favor for a friend," he explained. "An item of intrigue, of no particular importance."

He felt Hope's stare upon him, but he didn't acknowledge it. He needed Reeves to be willing to help him, and for no reason other than his own curiosity.

"Very well," Reeves said. "Tell me, how have you been?"

His blue stare pierced Anthony's face, and he felt like he was seven years old again. Part of him nearly told Reeves all that he was feeling – how much he longed to restore his family's name, how he didn't feel worthy enough to offer it to anyone else – but not only did he refuse to allow himself to revisit that line of thought, but he didn't want Hope to hear any of it.

It was the first time he had seen Reeves since the death of his father, and he was rather chilled at how all of the memories came flooding back.

"I have been well," he said slowly. "Mother is returning to herself again. She is actually visiting with Hope's mother at the moment. They're friends from childhood. It has been good to see."

"Glad to hear it," Reeves said, glancing over at Hope, and he knew what Reeves wanted to discuss.

"You can say what you would like to in front of Hope. I trust her."

Her head turned to him so swiftly that he wondered if she hurt herself, but it was true. He did trust her – with anything besides his own emotions – and was fine with hearing what Reeves had to say.

"I'm assuming you would like to speak about my father."

"I have to admit that I was becoming quite curious when I

hadn't heard from you as of late," Reeves said, fixing him with that pointed look that always had Anthony slightly worried.

"I have not been home as much as I would like recently, but, of course, I have not forgotten what we are searching for."

"Have you come any closer to the truth?" Reeves asked.

"I have not made much progress recently," Anthony admitted. "I have been preoccupied."

"I'm sorry to hear that," Reeves said in his low, rumbling voice, leaning forward to place his elbows upon his thighs. "But I have taken a closer look at the code that he was given to break."

"And?"

"I believe that he was entrapped. When the letters ended up in your father's hands, he solved an unbreakable code. The only way it could have been deduced was if he had been in possession of a cipher – one that had to have come from the French themselves."

"Right, that is what condemned him. It's also what I could never understand – how he had been in possession of it to start. He always said he received it anonymously."

"I believe he was given it in order to place blame upon him," Reeves said. "Whoever did so must have been the one working with the French, and when the investigation came too close, he decided to make it seem that it was your father instead."

Anthony scooted forward. "So why didn't Father try harder to prove himself?"

"Because he didn't want to cause any issues for you and your mother. He thought it best to simply live with it and hoped that it would all be forgotten."

"He thought better of them than they deserved, for no

one has ever forgotten," Anthony said bitterly. "How are we ever to prove them wrong?"

"You have to find the true traitor," Hope said suddenly, surprising them both. "And prove it."

"If it was that simple," Anthony began with some frustration, "then—"

"She's right," Reeves interjected, holding up a hand to stop Anthony. "We have always considered it, but we never took any steps forward. Your father didn't want us to. He said he had no wish to ruin another family's name."

"But it would have been the truth," Anthony said, annoyed.

Reeves shrugged. "You know how he was. Kind-hearted to a fault."

"Too kind-hearted for a brilliant man," Anthony muttered. "He forgot that his self-sacrifice also changed my mother's life. And my own."

"Now you are free to do something about it," Reeves said, leaning forward. "I am not sure where to start, but first do you want to tell me about why you are here? Show me what you have, and then we can determine how long you will be staying."

Anthony nodded, reaching for his bag beside him – the small one that he didn't think he would ever allow to be apart from him – and pulling out the two books. After he had removed them from their exterior binding, he had bound them in plain leather. He unfolded them on the scarred oak table before them, placing them side by side.

Reeves, his interest obviously piqued, walked over to the side of the room, sliding on gloves before he returned and ran his hands over the pages.

"Beautiful books," he whispered, obviously more to himself than to Anthony and Hope. "The ink and the coloring are immaculate. Attention to detail, craftsmanship, first rate."

"Yes," Anthony said, allowing Reeves to have the moment to appreciate the beauty before him. He understood it, even if he was eager to move on.

"What have you found so far?" Reeves asked.

"I thought I had it solved," Anthony explained. "I discovered words underlined on pages that also included numbers. I thought the numbers corresponded to pages and lines in the second book. However, all of the words or letters that I have found do not make any sense. That either isn't the code, or I am doing something wrong. I was hoping you could help."

"Where did you find the books?" Reeves asked.

"The first book we found as the answer to a riddle that our friends solved. They thought it would lead to treasure, but instead, only found this book. It came with a note that read, *'Greetings, my dear friend! It was such a pleasure to see you again. There is nothing new to report. I look forward to spending some time with you when I come to town this summer. Until then, cordially yours, friend.'* Then the Duke of Sheffield recalled that he had seen a nearly identical book at Newfield Manor – which is Hope's home. Her father was in possession of this second book, which his grandmother had been gifted by a friend in her youth."

"That is all very intriguing," Reeves said, before sitting back. "We shall look closer at them this evening. First, why do we not have something to eat? I have stew prepared over the cookstove as well as some bread, if that will suffice."

Anthony nodded, knowing, if nothing had changed, that Reeves had a woman come in daily to help him, as he didn't feel comfortable in having any staff live with him. He likely could have lived in a far greater estate due to his familial connections, but he always said he preferred it out here, alone.

Anthony hoped he wouldn't mind having their company for the night.

"I have a room prepared for you," Reeves said, as though reading Anthony's thoughts. "I suppose that will be for the lady now. You will have to sleep on the sofa."

"Thank you, Reeves. It is very kind of you to share your space, especially when I arrived unexpectedly," Hope said with a small smile. Reeves nodded at her, obviously taken by her charm. Not many people could crack his rigid exterior, but Hope, of course, had done so.

They made their way out to the small dining table and spent the majority of the meal reminiscing about Anthony's father. Reeves had a good number of stories, both about their work in the war effort as well as their days together as children.

"I haven't heard many of those anecdotes," Anthony said, sitting back and lifting his drink to his lips.

Reeves shrugged. "Your father preferred not to speak of some of them," he said. "He was a humble man and rarely claimed his accomplishments."

"This is true," Anthony said. "I think it was a broken heart that killed him, as he could never quite overcome the fact that the country he worked so hard for was the very one that turned on him."

"There is a lot of truth to that," Reeves said, and when Anthony looked up, he saw Hope peering at him intently, a sheen of water covering her eyes, and he was instantly annoyed with himself for bringing such a melancholy topic upon them all.

"Should we return to the books?" Anthony asked, attempting to clear the mood, and Reeves nodded as he stood, while Hope began to clear the table.

"I will do that," Reeves said, but Hope shook her head with a smile.

"I am capable. I think," she said with a bit of a laugh. "But it is best that the two of you begin your work."

When the table was clean, Reeves covered it with a sheet, and then set the books down upon it while he and Anthony donned their gloves.

Anthony lost track of time as the two of them worked into the night, reviewing every word, every letter, every number – anything they could think of while Hope sat in a corner of the sofa, her legs curled beneath her, a blanket over her as she read.

"I think I've found something," Reeves finally said, breaking the silence, and Anthony sat up expectantly.

"What is it?"

"A pattern – perhaps. Do not get too excited just yet. I think you were on to something, however, Anthony. You were just not reading it right."

"What are you thinking?"

"The combination of letters and numbers seems strange because it is an old form of Latin," Reeves explained. "I have hardly ever seen Old Latin in use before, but there was no difference in letter case."

"All right," Anthony said, waiting for him to continue. He noticed Hope had set aside her book and had now wandered over to listen, stopping behind Anthony's chair, one hand upon the back.

"Now, in this case, I believe there is a pattern to the letters, which I've figured out from the numbers," Reeves said.

Anthony was momentarily distracted when Hope leaned closer and the scent of lemons wafted through the air around him.

"By that, I mean that some of the numbers come after a

certain letter," Reeves continued. "Sometimes it is a single letter, sometimes it is more than one. But I think that if we took those letters and arranged them in a certain sequence, it would then form words."

Excitement built in Anthony's chest, and he sat forward in his chair, staring at the page that Reeves had turned to. "And then the message that accompanied the first book – would that point us to how to find the pattern?"

"I believe so," Reeves said, pulling the paper out and regarding the message written upon it once more.

Anthony felt Hope move behind him, her hand coming to rest on his shoulder as she bent forward, taking a closer look. Reeves continued to point out each word, each letter and number, as they began to work out the next set of words.

"There's a name," Hope said, pointing to a combination of letters. "It is a woman's name I believe."

"Mariana," Reeves said.

"I wonder if that is the name of one of Cassandra and Gideon's ancestors," Hope mused, placing a finger against her lips. "Part of their family is Spanish."

Anthony sat back as he tried to piece everything together. "I think I see a pattern now."

Hope rushed to get a quill as Reeves pointed out the next sequence of words and letters.

Anthony watched as she lay them out, and he could soon sense her excitement.

"Is it a poem?" he asked, but she was already shaking her head.

"No," she said. "It's a song. I recognize the words."

Reeves and Anthony looked at one another with a frown.

"But if it is a known song," Anthony said, drawing his brows together, "then why would they make such an effort to hide it?"

Reeves looked as bewildered as he felt. Hope held out the

paper and encouraged them to take it as she sang the words, her voice echoing through the room.

Anthony could pick out the tune, but the words didn't seem to make any sense.

But her voice captivated him just as much as the woman herself, her music filling him with peace as it had at Castleton. Peace that he welcomed as much as it frightened him.

For he wasn't entirely sure what to do about it.

CHAPTER 16

"*Mariana, mi amor, has llenado mi corazón. Me ha dejado tan ligero y sintiendo calor.*"

Hope sang the tune again softly as she prepared for bed. The room was as humble as the rest of the cottage, but it was comfortable, and she appreciated Reeves allowing her to stay, despite the fact that he had not expected her, nor, according to Anthony, was he usually comfortable with strangers. She turned back the blankets and was about to snuggle between them when there was a light knock on the door. Her heartrate increased as she walked toward it, knowing who she would find on the other side.

"Anthony," she said softly when she found him standing there. He had been running his hands through his hair for the majority of the evening while studying the books, and it was rather dishevelled now, hanging down around his forehead. He had already removed his jacket, cravat, and waistcoat, and Hope decided she rather liked how he looked in only his trousers and linen shirt, a few buttons open at the collar.

"I was hoping to catch you before you retired for the

night," he said, stepping backward, actually appearing some-what hesitant. "But if you are in need of sleep—"

"It's fine," she said, opening the door wider. "Will Reeves be scandalized to know you are in here?"

"I can hear his snores from the hall," he said with a small chuckle. "We should be fine."

Once he was within the room, he paced slowly back and forth, and Hope sat on a corner of the bed, waiting patiently for him to get to the point he was here to make.

"What do you think it means?"

Hope tried to push away the disappointment that filled her at his words. She hadn't realized how much she had been hoping that he was here to see her – and for more reasons than to talk about this never-ending clue.

"*Mariana, my love, has filled my heart. She has left me so light and feeling warmth,* is essentially what it means," she murmured. "It's a love song, about the love a man has for a woman," she said. "It begins with him believing that he cannot have her, but in the end they find a way to be together."

"A happy love song. How rare," he said.

"I prefer happy songs."

"I am baffled as to how the song can have anything to do with this treasure hunt," he said, and Hope tapped a finger against her lips.

"I have an idea, actually."

"You do?" he said, spinning around quickly, and Hope had to hold back her smile at the excitement that covered his face. He was so sullen most of the time that when he did show another emotion, it was far more fulfilling to see.

"I do," she confirmed. "What if it is not the *words* of the song, but the notes?"

"What do you mean?"

"Maybe together in a sequence they will provide a

pattern, one that could lead to us solving the clue," she said, twisting her hands together as she wondered whether he would think that her idea was foolish. "Or perhaps they might lead to a message in the books?"

He stopped, hands on his hips as he stared at her, his eyes widening, his face brightening in what Hope could only describe as akin to joy – an emotion she had hardly ever seen on Anthony.

"Hope," he breathed. "That is—that is genius." He rushed over toward her, his hands gently gripping her upper arms as he lifted her up, and before she even realized what was happening, his arms were wrapped around her and he was spinning her around the room. She laughed at his exhilaration, and when he finally placed her back on her feet in front of him, she was breathless – and for more reason than being sent in circles.

"I could kiss you right now," he said, the smile still on his lips, and Hope realized that she would like that more than anything.

"Then do so," she said, swallowing hard as his eyes lost their glee and became heavy and hooded.

"I—"

He seemed frozen to the spot, and Hope didn't think she could stand for him to deny her, so before he could do so, she stood on her toes, leaned forward, and pressed her lips against his. He froze for a moment before he responded to her with even more intensity, his mouth hard and unrelenting as he did more than accept her kiss. His arms, still around her, pressed her close against him, and Hope wound her hands into his hair, craving him with the same need as to breathe.

The kiss seemed to last an eternity, each of them drinking in the other's presence with complete abandon. As their lips moved together, she began to remember the night before and the whisper of his breath on her neck, the warmth of his body pressed against hers, and the way that he had whispered her name.

When the kiss finally ended, they leaned back and looked at each other with a mixture of surprise, confusion, and longing. In that moment, nothing else mattered, and the world seemed to stand still. All that existed was the two of them. No riddle, no past, no secrets, and no family forbidding them from one another.

Hope had taken her hair out of its pins and plaited most of it, but tendrils had loosened around her face and Anthony now tucked one behind her ear, his eyes solemn and serious as he stared deeply into her eyes. Hope's breath caught and her entire body was filled with need – for him. She wasn't sure how to tell him so, but then he seemed to decide for her as he lifted her up and then placed her back on the bed. His arms framed her head as he kissed her again, and Hope found herself opening to him, accepting whatever it was he wanted to give her – or take. For she wasn't sure what it was about him that so called to her, but she couldn't help but want to return that joy to him once more.

"Hope," he murmured, before leaning down and kissing her again. She arched up toward him, knowing what she wanted but unsure if she should take it.

"Anthony," she whispered, evoking the same response.

His hands cupped her hips, lifting her as he slowly slid the nightgown up her body, his fingers stroking her calves, her knees, her thighs. Then his hands were on her waist, and he stopped for a moment, fingers digging into her flesh.

"What it is?" she asked breathily.

"You're beautiful." He kissed her again, before nibbling down her neck until her collarbone, and she jumped slightly when his hand cupped her breast. He lifted his head, looking down at her before he asked, "Do you trust me?"

"Yes," she whispered. "I shouldn't, but… I do."

"Everyone in your life will tell you that you shouldn't," he said, and then brushed a light kiss across her lips. "And they're right. I am not the man for you. I cannot give you what you need for your future. But I can give you what you need right now."

She wanted to ask just what he meant by that, why he considered himself unworthy, but then their gazes met and the thrumming between her legs became more insistent than any other question.

"Which is?" she managed, her voice barely more than a whisper.

"I will not make love to you, for I cannot ruin you like that. But, if you let me, I will make you feel things you have never felt before."

A low moan escaped her throat in response, and then he was moving down her body, his lips leading the way.

"Anthony?" she said, questioning, her pulse quickening, but he ignored her as his strong hands came to her thighs, lifting them so that her legs were wrapped around his shoulders. Before she had time to completely realize what he was doing, he leaned in and flattened his tongue against her, the sensation so strong that Hope jumped. He reached up, tracing his hands down her arms until he gripped one of her hands within his, as comforting as any caress could be. His tongue continued to move against her center until Hope forgot all of her worries, all of her reservations, as all she could focus on was his tongue against her, his hand covering hers, and his other fingers which now reached below his mouth and were massaging her from within.

Hope's body became fluid, relaxing into Anthony and all he was doing to her as his mouth moved faster, until, as much as it was the best she had ever felt, she also wasn't sure how much longer she could take it.

Anthony continued to work her with his tongue, and Hope arched her back, unknowing when this would end and whether or not she wanted it to. She laced her fingers through his hair as she had before, but this time she tugged on it, asking him for something but unsure just what it was.

He kept her open as he continued until, just when she was on the brink of collapse, waves of pleasure began running through her, as it seemed like her soul had come apart from her body and was floating above her.

When she finally opened her eyes and came back to herself, Anthony was planting kisses up her thighs, until he pulled her nightgown down over top of her legs and settled himself on the bed next to her as Hope tried to catch her breath.

It took a moment for her to turn her head to look at him, unsure if she should be embarrassed or... completely satisfied.

"How are you?" he asked lowly, meeting her eyes, his simple, caring question bringing tears to Hope's eyes and ridding her of all of her reservations.

"I am... wonderful," she said, her answer bringing a small, smirking smile to his face, and she realized that he had been worried about her response.

"Good," he said, his tone light. "That was my aim."

The languid comfort that had spread through Hope's body slowly began to dissipate as she became very aware that Anthony hadn't received anything out of this... and if he said he wasn't going to make love to her, then did he expect something else from her? Panic gripped her as, despite the books and conversations she and her friends secretly enjoyed, she had no idea just what she was supposed to do.

"Anthony, I—"

Somehow, he seemed to understand what she was think-ing, for he turned to her and traced a finger down her cheek.

"That was for you. I need nothing in return."

"But—"

He shook his head against the blankets. "I know I shouldn't have done that but…" He looked away for a moment, and Hope saw the tick of his jaw, the slightest of red coloring his cheeks. "You do something to me," he muttered, and Hope raised herself on an elbow to look at him, but he wouldn't meet her gaze anymore.

"I never meant to…" she began, but he shook his head.

"Of course you didn't. It's not your fault. It's mine," he said. "I should have had more restraint. I should have—"

"Anthony." Hope could hardly believe that she was the one providing reassurance. She had never seen this side of him before – a vulnerable side, that showed her there was more beneath the prickly exterior he presented to the world. "I will remember that forever. Thank you."

CHAPTER 17

*A*s much as he was no innocent youth in his first sexual encounter, Anthony had some difficulty looking Hope in the eye the next morning.

It was not so much what they had done – make that, what *he* had done – but what had come afterward. He had allowed her to see how affected he was, how much she made him *feel*. At one point, she was practically consoling him.

It was the very reason he never should have done what he did. He was in too deep.

But he couldn't have properly described the sudden need to touch her, to taste her, to make her understand that she was his to take.

Even though it was all kinds of wrong.

The three of them sat together now at the breakfast table, Hope looking up at Anthony every now and then, her cheeks turning pink each time she did before she quickly lowered her head and returned her attention to the porridge in front of her. Reeves would be a fool not to sense that there was something between her and Anthony, and if there was one thing the man was not, it was stupid.

"What will you do now?" Reeves asked.

"If you don't mind, I thought we would remain here one more day, studying the books and making sure we have the clues solved correctly. We are also going to attempt your theory," Anthony said. He also wouldn't mind spending more time with the man who knew him better than anyone else on this earth save his mother, but he didn't want to say that aloud. "Then we can begin our return journey tomorrow."

"Very well," Reeves said. "You are welcome to stay as long as you wish."

"Thank you, Reeves," Hope said softly, smiling at him and he nodded in return before looking between the two of them. "I think, if it is all right, I shall take a walk in the woods around the house while you work?"

"Of course," Reeves said, and Anthony had to fight every inclination to stand up and follow after her, trailing her every step to make sure she was safe. "She'll be fine," Reeves murmured as they watched her clean her bowl and then slip out the door.

When Anthony turned back to Reeves to discuss their plan for the day, he found the man staring at him with a smug grin on his face.

"It's not what you think," Anthony said tersely.

"Isn't it, though?" Reeves said, winging up an eyebrow. "I do not need to be a codebreaker to deduce that there is something between the two of you."

"We are friendly," Anthony said, busying himself by cleaning off the table so that they might shortly commence.

"I did not want to say it in front of the lady, but she's clearly ruined now, having travelled alone with you."

Anthony sighed as he gave up the pretense and sat back down in his chair, crossing one leg over the other knee as he turned to Reeves.

"That's what I told her when she asked to accompany me.

Apparently, she didn't trust me with her father's book, but I told her it was impossible for us to journey together. Then she created this elaborate plan and stowed away in my carriage."

"How is that even possible?" Reeves asked, and by the time Anthony finished telling him the story, he was laughing.

"That is rich."

"I suppose."

"And now?"

"Well, now we shall see if her plan works."

Reeves sobered as he stared at Anthony, his clear blue eyes intent. "Would you marry her if you had to?"

Anthony ran his hand over his trousers before meeting Reeves' eye. "You know I would if I had no other choice. I do have some honor."

"But?"

"But I do not feel that I am in a position to offer marriage to *any* young lady. Besides, her father is well aware of my family's circumstances and has no interest in seeing his daughter with a man like me. I have been warned off multiple times. And that was before I broke into his study and stole his book."

"Alone?"

"With Hope's help," Anthony amended. "Actually, this is the second time I've compromised her, for her father found us alone in his study in the middle of the night. But he would rather risk her ruination than see her with me."

"And yet now you have stolen both his book and his daughter."

"Borrowed."

"Very well."

Reeves studied him so intently that Anthony had to look away.

"You know that your father wouldn't want you to live like this, paying for sins that he didn't even commit."

"It wasn't his fault. Not entirely," Anthony said, not saying what he truly felt – that if only his father had fought for the truth, it might have all turned out differently.

"If we could prove his innocence now and restore your family name," Reeves began, cocking his head to the side, "would you marry a woman like Lady Hope? If not Lady Hope herself?"

Anthony paused the bobbing of his foot up and down. He hadn't allowed himself to think like that, to get too far ahead. He knew what he had done with her was wrong, but nothing in his life had ever felt so right before. She fit him. She brought out parts of himself that he hadn't known existed. And she was still here, despite how many times he had told her that she shouldn't be caught with him.

"Yes," he said slowly. "Yes, if her father was not opposed, I suppose I would."

"Well, then," Reeves said, clapping his hands against his leg. "Enough of this codebreaking business. We have a mystery to solve."

* * *

HOPE WAS surprised when Anthony told her not to pack her things just yet.

He asked to speak with her after dinner that evening, and they sat together on the sofa in front of the fire as Hope picked at one of the errant threads on a cushion.

"Would you mind staying another couple of days?" he asked. "I suppose the better question is how that will line up with your supposed return."

"Actually, another couple of days should be fine," she said, somewhat relieved, for she had been wondering how to

ELLIE ST. CLAIR

approach this with him. "I sent a message to Faith, and I hoped to hear back before we returned so I would know when and where to meet her." She cocked her head as she studied him, feeling that there was something he wasn't telling her. "Why the sudden urge to stay? If you would like more time to visit with Reeves, I completely understand."

"It's not that," he said, shaking his head.

"Do we not already have our next clue? I feel that it will be the ultimate wedding gift for Cassandra. I can hardly wait to share the news."

"Wedding?" he said, frowning at her. "Goodness, I forgot all about that."

"Yes!" she exclaimed, unable to hide her surprise. "We must be at Castleton within three weeks for Cassandra and Devon's nuptials. It slipped your mind?"

"I have been thinking of… other things," he said, his gaze suddenly turning dark and hooded as it had the night before and suddenly, Hope was shivering once more, in much of an anticipatory way.

"Well," she said, looking down at her hands as her face warmed all over again, "I believe your mother had planned to travel from Newfield Manor directly there, so perhaps we shall be travelling companions again."

"This time, I shall be riding my horse," he muttered so darkly that she couldn't help but laugh.

"That makes perfect sense, given how the carriage makes you ill," she said. "Is there anything I can do to help?"

"Nothing," he said, shaking his head, his eyes distant once more. "Unfortunately, your theory does not seem to work, although the notes could mean something still. Actually, Reeves and I also want to further discuss who could have possibly set up my father. It is rather unlikely we will find anything, but I have nothing to lose in trying to find an answer."

"Of course. If I can help in any way, I am happy to do so."
She paused and when he didn't take her up on her offer, she
continued. "I believe I shall retire now," she said, standing,
uncertain exactly of what she should say, if she should issue
him an invitation to come to her again. For, as much as she
knew she shouldn't, she would not be opposed to another
late-night visit from him. In fact, she hadn't been able to stop
thinking about him and how he had made her feel. Now she
finally understood why Cassandra had allowed Devon to
take her innocence those years ago, and then welcomed him
to her bed once more.

She was still perplexed by her feelings toward Anthony,
how the surly gruff viscount had become the man she
couldn't stop thinking about, even before they had departed
on this journey together. Had he been any other man, she'd
have turned him away before he even stepped foot in her
bedroom. But she hadn't been able to prevent herself from
letting him in.

Why did he have to be the man whom her father forbade
her from even speaking to, the man who told her that he had
nothing to offer her?

It was all a web of confusion that Hope had no idea how
to escape.

What scared her the most was that she rather liked having
been caught.

CHAPTER 18

*A*nthony spent the next two nights sleeping on the sofa, staring at the door of Hope's bedroom, wondering if she was also thinking of him.

In truth, he wasn't certain why she would besides the fact that he was there. He was sure that there were many other gentlemen she would prefer – gentlemen who not only had something to offer her, but who were much more pleasant and charming, men she would actually want to spend time with.

He had forced himself to stay well away from her. For he knew that if he entered her bedroom again, he might not stop at just pleasuring her. She was too tempting, and every time she lifted her beautiful face to look at him, or her hand stroked his arm, or her lips turned up in that beautiful bow of a pink smile, he fell a little deeper for her.

He wasn't the man for her, but he also knew that he would have to be careful moving forward – for he wasn't sure how he would react if he was present and saw her with another man. A woman like her was sure to attract more attention.

But at the moment, that shouldn't be his concern. In fact, he shouldn't even be thinking of her. He should be thinking of the strides that he and Reeves had made in proving his father's innocence. They had begun to determine what evidence they would require – his father's whereabouts, his loyalties, the fact he had no reason to work with the French. They also had to prove that he had never been financially compensated.

They had spent a great deal of time discussing who might have had something to gain from a traitorous allegiance against their country – and who knew Anthony's father's activities well enough to have sent the cipher to him.

"To me, there is only one true suspect," Anthony finally said over breakfast the day they planned to leave. Anthony and Reeves hadn't prevented themselves from speaking of the subject in front of Hope, but he had asked his father's old friend not to say anything about *why* it had suddenly become imperative that they discover who was truly the traitor.

"Who?" Reeves asked.

"His handler – the man who provided the two of you with the letters," he said. "They almost always came through him, did they not, unless it was an urgent message delivered to him directly from the front?"

"You think it was Johnson?"

"Yes."

"I'm not sure," Reeves said slowly. "I'd have thought that he was as loyal of a man there ever was."

"How well did you truly know him?" Anthony pressed.

"I see why you would suspect him," Reeves said. "But if it is him, we must be very careful, as he knows people in high places. How would we ever prove it?"

"That's the question," Anthony said.

Eventually they decided that Anthony would pay a visit to Lieutenant Johnson when he returned to London, but that wouldn't be for a time – not until after Cassandra and Devon's wedding.

While they conversed, Anthony couldn't help watching Hope, who was moving about the cottage, packing up any of her things that were lying about. He didn't miss her straightening the cottage as she did so, and neither did Reeves. While Hope was occupied, he leaned in, his voice low.

"Good luck with her, Anthony. And if nothing else, remember your father's greatest lesson – that sometimes you must put the happiness of yourself and your loved ones above all else. It's what he thought he was doing. Do you hear me?"

"I do," he said, mostly to placate the man, before he and Hope issued Reeves their final farewells before boarding the carriage to leave.

Hope let out a small sigh as they rolled away.

"What's wrong?" Anthony asked.

"It's silly," she said, looking down and to the side.

"Now you have to tell me."

"I suppose I was just thinking about how I shall miss our time here. It was so peaceful. I've never been anywhere that there weren't servants nearly always at my elbow, ready to leap to fulfill my every wish. I'd have thought that I would miss them, but I felt rather useful while we were here."

"There is some comfort in solitude," he agreed. "But after a time, I am sure you would decide that you prefer the comforts of home."

"Perhaps," she said, before they lapsed into silence once more. This time, instead of an awkward discomfort, it was an easy silence, one that Anthony could sink into.

"Did you hear from Faith?" he said a few minutes later, and Hope winced, worrying Anthony.

"I did."

"And?"

"She said she would meet us at the inn in Bures. Where we stopped on the way here. I never told her of our overnight visit, but she must have determined what our schedule would be. It takes her slightly away from her journey, but she agreed it would be best."

"What else did she say?"

Hope's face was not exactly the picture of innocence as she asked, "what do you mean?"

"What did your sister have to say about your little escapade?"

"Oh, that," Hope said, swallowing, her neck bobbing as she did. "She wasn't exactly... pleased."

Anthony snorted. "I do not suppose she was. Her innocent little sister, all alone with a man like me."

Hope's eyes widened as she looked at him from across the seat, where she was perched on the edge.

"I can handle myself."

"I am well aware of that," he said, shifting closer toward her, unable to help himself. She drew him to her like a horse to water.

"Then why—" She stopped, looking away. "Never mind."

"Continue."

"Why didn't you come back?" she asked, her words a whisper, her eyes wide and staring, as though haunted that she had even dared to ask such a question. Anthony didn't have to ask to what she was referring. She was asking him why he hadn't returned to her at night after the first time between them.

"I couldn't," he said in a low voice, wishing she would forget the subject, but instead she leaned even farther forward.

"What do you mean?"

Anthony groaned as he rubbed his temples between his thumbs and forefingers.

"If I had come to you," he began, speaking from between gritted teeth. He shouldn't be saying this to her, but she deserved an explanation. "I likely would not have been able to stop where I did last time."

"What are you saying?" she asked, her blue eyes wide, and Anthony had to look away.

"We should not be speaking of this," he said, as he felt all the blood in his body rush to his growing erection, and he shifted in his seat to try to hide it.

"Nor should I be here alone with you, nor should you have entered my bedroom the other night," she returned, one eyebrow cocked in a way that had his heart pounding with a deep rhythm that urged him forward. "Yet here we are."

"Very well," he growled. "If you really must know... if I had returned, I just might have made love to you, truly ruining you for all others."

She dipped her head before returning her gaze to his, vulnerability in her eyes now.

"Perhaps... perhaps that wouldn't be such a bad thing," she whispered.

"Hope," he began again, "I have told you before that I cannot marry you – at least not right now. Besides..." he didn't want to ask, had to choke out the words, but he needed to know, "why would you even want to?"

"Because," she said, scooting even farther forward so that she was on the edge of her seat and it was a wonder she didn't fall off. She reached her hand out tentatively and placed it on his knee, "I have always found you to be an attractive man. You are brooding, yes, but it is somehow endearing. It seems to me that you are hiding your true feelings behind that prickly exterior. And as I have come to know you, I have realized that there is more to you than you let on. It was obvious from when you first came to stay with us just how much you care about your mother and would do anything for her. But there is more than that. You also clearly care about Gideon, if you are willing to do this for him, even when you obviously had no wish to. And I believe that part of the reason you wanted to stay was because you wanted to spend more time with Reeves."

He dipped his head abashedly. "I did enjoy seeing him again."

"And you have been most considerate toward me," she said, her lips curling slightly, enticing him all the more. "Even when my father and Faith have both been unkind, and I have made things quite difficult for you. You could have thrown me out of this carriage onto my bottom the moment you discovered me, and yet, here we are."

"I must admit something to you," he said slowly, and her fingers tightened their grip upon his thigh.

"Yes?"

"I am terrified to see your sister."

She laughed then, tilting her head backward, exposing the long column of her neck. It was hard to believe that he had ever been opposed to the joy she greeted life with. Now he didn't think he would ever tire of it; he only wished he could know what that was like. Perhaps the only way for him to truly discover it was to view it through her.

When her laughter settled, he found her face just inches from his, and his breath caught as he fought everything within him to lean forward and kiss her again. How many times had he told himself to stay away from her? But before he could process just what he was *supposed* to be doing, she leaned in and kissed him, stealing his breath away.

Her kiss began hesitantly, but her touch ignited a fire within him, one he had been attempting to tamp out, but the flames kept stubbornly flickering. Her one innocent kiss had him roaring up for her, as he reached out and wrapped his arms around her, lifting her off her seat and pulling her over to his side of the carriage. His tongue dove into her mouth, making love to it as he wanted to do to her with his body.

She paused for just a moment before she was fumbling with something behind his head, and he realized she was removing her gloves when her soft hands slipped around his neck, the firmness with which she gripped him surprising him. She shifted in his lap so that she was straddling him, her knees beside his thighs. There was so much clothing and fabric still between them that he wondered whether she could even feel anything – but then she rubbed up against him where he was hard. He reached for her and moaned.

That was the moment he truly came undone.

He didn't remember removing her clothes or any of his own, as all he was focused on was the feel of her mouth against his, of kissing her properly before running his lips down the skin of her neck that had been calling him, enticing him all day.

Then he noticed that all that was covering her breasts was the thin fabric of her chemise, as apparently, he had been unfastening the back of her gown while he had been kissing her. Her hands were at the top of his trousers, and he lifted his hips so that she could free him. Her eyes went wide as they flicked down toward him, and he couldn't help his throaty chuckle at her "my goodness!"

"That's your fault," he growled, leaning forward and kissing her over her collarbone until he found her breast, his tongue circling her nipple, and he heard her intake of breath as she arched into him.

He knew how incredibly lucky he was that she was trusting him with her body, though he wasn't sure he was worthy of that trust as she began to shift back and forth over his lap in rhythm with his mouth on her. If she didn't stop that soon, this was going to be over before it even began.

He tried to distract her by moving to her other nipple,

grazing it with his teeth as he cupped her breasts, which fit perfectly in his hands.

"I do not have the most, um, generous bosom," she said, and he looked up at her, reading the worry in her eyes.

"You are beautiful," he murmured. "As perfect as could be."

He took her lips again as his hands framed her hips before sliding up, over her ribs, back beneath her breasts to show her just how much he liked them. Her movements became more insistent, and he lifted her skirts up around her waist, fanning them out around them as he slid one hand within to cup her between her legs. As he returned his mouth to her breast, he began to stroke her bud of sensitivity, and she hissed out his name in a way that made him want to claim her, to tell all of the world that she was his and his alone.

"Anthony," she said again, pleading in her voice this time, "Can you... I need... I want... you," she finished, and he shook his head.

"You do not know what you're asking."

"I do," she said, certainty filling her eyes as she stared down at him. "I want to feel all of you."

She reached down then, finding him beneath her skirts, batting them out of the way endearingly before her hand wrapped around him, and he let out a groan as she slid it up and down.

"Inside," she said again, and he wasn't sure whether he should be grateful or damn those books she read that appeared to have taught her more than a woman like her should know about.

He reached down, gripped her hips, and lifted her then, until she was positioned just above his cock. He waited, giving her the power, and she slowly lowered herself down around him, gasping as she did so. She paused for a moment, rising slightly before lowering again, and Anthony gritted his teeth as he prevented himself from moving, even though all he wanted to do was lift and lower her, thrusting himself within.

"Are you all right?" he managed to ask, and she nodded, closing her eyes for a beat before opening them and staring at him.

"More than all right," she said, before moving back and forth, up and down upon him, and he leaned in to kiss her again, partially to distract himself from her movements. She was easily sliding up and down him now, and he held her close as he kept himself from letting go. It might take every ounce of will within him, but he wouldn't, not until she came.

His fingers played with her nipples, softly teasing them, and she leaned into him, moving faster now, as he began to thrust in time with her. She lifted her head, then, her blue eyes staring into his incredulously, her mouth slightly open in what he could only hope was pleasant surprise.

"Anthony," she breathed.

"Yes," he practically shouted, as he could no longer hold back and began pumping into her harder, realizing in the back of his mind that it had never been like this with another woman and likely never would again.

She began to squeeze him from inside, until she was pulsing around him as she threw her head back and cried out his name, urging his own release forward. With Herculean effort, he managed to hold off until she finished, and when she collapsed against him, he lifted her off him to the seat beside them and spent on the floor below.

When he turned to her, he was filled by the overwhelming need to take care of her, to ensure that she was all right, and he gently lifted an errant lock of her hair and tucked it behind her ear before kissing her again, needing her to know but unable to tell her just how much he cared for her, that this was different from any experience had ever been for him before.

But he was unable to find the right words, so instead he leaned in and kissed her gently once more before he cleaned up the carriage with his handkerchief and helped restore their clothing to rights.

"Should I... should I go back to my seat?" she asked, gesturing across, as though uncertain of just where this left them.

"No," he said fiercely. He didn't know what the future would hold for them, but for now, the only thing he knew for certain was that he couldn't let her go. "Stay right here with me."

He reached out, wrapped her within her arms and held her close, never in his life being both so completely content and yet absolutely terrified.

CHAPTER 19

a s they pulled into the inn in Bures, Hope glanced over at Anthony, wondering just how they were to approach their stay here once more.

"Faith is supposed to arrive tomorrow at noon," she said, toying with the edges of her skirts, which were now restored to rights. She knew that as a proper young lady she should be scandalized with both herself and Anthony for what they had just done, but she couldn't seem to conjure any emotion except contentment. What type of woman that made her, she had no idea, but she refused to allow herself to feel shamed for it. "Should we pose as a married couple again?"

When she managed enough courage to lift her eyes to Anthony, she noticed the intensity of his stare upon her, and her heart started racing again at the thought of a repetition of their actions. She had never before felt anything so tremendously triumphant, and she had an urge to chase that feeling again.

"I suppose," he murmured, "but if she arrives early…"

"She won't," Hope said assuredly. "Faith is nothing but punctual."

"Someone is becoming rather rebellious, now, isn't she?" he said with a grin unlike any expression she had ever seen upon him before, and when she let out a giggle, it was far too giddy for her own liking. Anthony, however, didn't seem to take any notice.

It wasn't long until they were in their room once more – the same one as they had previously resided — and Hope found herself as nervous as she had been the first time, although for entirely different reasons now.

Should they eat first? Would Anthony not want anything from her again, as she could imagine that their first time likely was not as pleasurable for him as it was for her, being that it had been *her* first time and he had likely had far better? Would he think she would expect something, even when she knew that he had no interest in—

"Hope," he said in his gravelly voice, stepping toward her and taking her chin between his thumb and index finger, lifting her head to look up at him, his grey eyes calm and searching. "I can practically hear you thinking. Just know that you need not be worried about whatever thoughts are running through your mind. I am happy if you are happy, and that is all you need to be concerned about."

Warmth bloomed through her chest at his care, and she figured it was at that moment that she completely fell for him – even though she knew that she absolutely should not.

They dined in a private room downstairs, their conversation easy, as Anthony seemed to have shifted to be much more comfortable with her, although now and again she caught him looking at her with this stare as though he was in some disbelief.

"What did you tell Faith in your letter?" he asked her, tilting his head, and she hated the fact that they would soon be returning to their usual world, the one in which they were not alone together in a carriage or pretending to be husband and wife as they shared a room in the inn.

"The truth, for the most part," she said. "Which will mean that I am the only one she should have issue with – not you."

"She will likely expect me to wed you based on the fact that we have been alone together for such a time," he said. "As will your father. And about that, Hope—"

"I know," she said, more abruptly than she intended to. Anthony had been nothing but honest with her, and there was no reason for her to get fanciful notions in her head. She had initiated their relations in the carriage, knowing full well what his intentions were. "This is all there will be between us."

He reached across the table and took her hand in his, his warm fingers stroking the top of her hand. "I do not wish for you to be upset. But even if your father did approve of the two of us, I cannot give you a sullied name."

"Well, it won't be for long," she said as brightly as she could, extracting her hand and then patting the top of his with as much cheerfulness as she could muster. "You will clear your family's name soon. Not that I would expect anything even if you did," she added hastily, and he smiled wanly at her, joy not quite reaching his eyes.

"Are you finished eating?"

"I am," she said, having lost her appetite, even though, as before, it tasted as good as anything the cook at home would have made, although it was certainly lacking in presentation.

"Should we go upstairs, then?" he asked, his voice dropping an octave.

Silently, she nodded.

"I do not expect anything, Hope," he added quickly.

She softly replied, "I know," for she actually did. But perhaps she had longings of her own.

He was the gentleman again, stepping outside while she

readied for bed, even though she told him that was ridiculous, given what he'd seen, touched, and tasted of her. He was insistent that she have time to herself, however, which she appreciated.

And when she slid into the covers, she had a surprise for him – one that had her heart thumping, as she wondered if she was being far too forward, knowing how humiliated she would be if he rejected her.

Anthony was still dressed in his shirt and trousers when he got into bed, and Hope suddenly wondered if she had expected too much, lying there frozen beside him as her thoughts began to race once more. Could she slip out of bed and set everything to rights? Was he aware of what she had done? Would—

"Hope?"

"Yes," she squeaked.

"Are you—are you wearing anything?"

"Umm…"

If she said yes, would he believe her lie? But that was ridiculous, for obviously he was only asking because he had already noticed. She took a breath. She never should have kissed him in the carriage, never should have begun this journey that had led to her fanciful notions. Damn those books. She blamed Cassandra for all of this, for if she had never started their stupid book club, then Hope never would have read any of those romantic books, and never would have thought—

Oh, goodness. Anthony's lips were on her neck. His hand on her hip. And—yes. That was the hard length of him pressing against her bottom. Perhaps she hadn't been so wrong in her imaginings after all.

"Hope," he murmured.

"Yes?" she said, and goodness, why did her voice go so high when that yearning overwhelmed her again?

"Was this purposeful?"

"Yes."

"Good," he said, rolling her over until he was hovering on top of her. "I seem to recall that you set the pace last time."

She could only nod, as she had lost her voice from the intensity in his eyes, the way he looked at her like he was about to devour her.

"My turn," was all he said before he dipped his head and began to kiss her, his lips this time not as fast and furious as they had been in the carriage, but now slow and languid, which seemed to cause her bones to melt and her body to sink into the mattress below her.

She was at the mercy of his mouth, which had left her lips and was now traversing down her body, leaving a trail of fire as it ran over her shoulders, collarbones, and breasts. He spent some time with both of her nipples, leaving her arching up into him, ready for more.

"You are wearing far too many clothes," she said as she wrapped her hand around his neck, holding him close against her.

"That is one problem I can solve," he said gruffly, before sitting up and stripping in front of her, offering a fine view of sinewy, lean muscle, and a light dusting of hair over his chest that ran in a line down beneath his trousers — a line she followed with her finger, stopping at his waistband. Then with a deep breath for courage, she began to undo his fastenings, and he helped her slip off his trousers.

Her breath caught at the sight of him, but this time she had prior knowledge – that he was able to fit. More than fit. He was the perfect size to allow her to feel everything she longed for once more.

His head dipped, and his tongue began to swirl against her, causing her to buck up off the bed, tears forming in her eyes as, even while she loved this more than she could properly explain, she was already sad at the thought that this might be her last opportunity to be with him like this again.

She pulled him up and he paused at her entrance, staring at her with a whispered, "are you all right?" as he must have seen her tears. She nodded, urging him forward, and he slowly slid into her with a groan.

His movements this time began as slow and unhurried as his kisses had, as though he was also aware that he must savor this. Before long, however, as their desire for one another grew in a crescendo, neither of them could hold back, and when Hope closed her eyes and allowed the rainbow of light and warmth to wash over her, he stilled before pulling out and spending on the sheet next to them.

This time, after he tenderly cleaned her up and tugged her into his arms, Hope could not turn off the thoughts that flooded her. The thoughts that pictured the two of them together like this, every night and every morning.

Thoughts that she would will away later.

But for now, she would simply enjoy.

CHAPTER 20

*A*nthony had never been the most obedient of children. He had preferred to do as he pleased, even if it meant going against the rules that had been set before him. He had never been particularly worried about the consequences nor the disappointment he might meet.

But now, as he sat in the hard, scarred, straight-back chair in the inn's dining room watching Lady Faith Newfield walk through the front door, he felt as though he was a guilty child waiting for his nursemaid to mete out punishment.

Lady Faith's face was pinched in anger – and perhaps some worry – as her eyes set on him and Hope, who sat across from him with her hands folded in her lap.

"Why do you look so guilty?" Hope asked him in a loud whisper, to which his eyes flicked over toward her.

"Because I *am* guilty."

"Well, don't let her know that!"

Anthony hastily stood when Lady Faith reached their table, his chair falling over behind him at his urgency. She crossed her arms over her chest and stared him down, causing him to swallow hard.

"What do you have to say for yourself?" she asked before issuing a greeting as she crossed her arms, and Anthony stuttered as he searched for a reply.

"Pardon me?"

"Faith," Hope interjected, stepping forward between them, "Anthony did nothing wrong. This was all my doing, as I explained to you in the letter."

"*Anthony?*" Faith repeated, turning to her sister with wide eyes. "Is that not rather familiar?"

"Faith," Hope said firmly. "This was my decision. And, as it happens, it was a good one. For we were able to solve the clue. That will be the best wedding gift for Cassandra, will it not?" She fixed a smile to her face that Anthony knew he would never be able to deny, but apparently Faith was impervious to it.

"You are compromised now. You do know that," she stated, staring her sister down, but Hope kept that smile fixed to her face.

"I do not have to be," she said calmly. "You are the only one who knows of my deception. If you say nothing, all will be well."

"What about Percy and her family? They might say something to Mother."

"Did you tell Percy of the situation?"

"Yes."

"Will she keep the secret?"

"Of course."

"I thought her mother was out visiting her own mother," Hope said with a smile that would have been devious on any other but was still rather sweet on her.

"She was..."

"Then all will be well," Hope said brightly, although Faith did not appear convinced.

"These things have a way of getting out."

She was right about that, but Anthony didn't have any wish to disappoint Hope at the moment.

"Faith," Hope said, reaching out and placing a hand on her arm. "Do *you* promise to keep this secret? For now, at least?"

Lady Faith stilled as she looked from one of them to the other. "I will not tell anyone of what has happened, but nor will I deny it if I am asked about it."

Hope pressed her lips together. "That is all that I can ask for."

"If Father finds out—" Lady Faith's look of warning was directed at Anthony once more, but he was prepared for this. He nodded in agreement.

He did not want to be married, could not offer much. But if he was pressed, he would marry her. For he was beginning to realize that he would do practically anything for Hope. He just prayed he'd have time to set all to rights first.

* * *

THEIR RETURN to Newfield Manor had, so far, gone according to plan. Hope rode with Faith the rest of the way, stopping to pick up her maid. They had to bribe the ladies' maids to keep the secret, although they shared with them the story that Hope had been to see another of their friends and had met them at the inn. Hope was aware that the story was now so complicated that she might have a hard time remembering the various threads of the deception. It made her rather nervous, but she was too deep into this now.

She had done what she had to do, and the books remained safe.

Anthony followed a few hours behind them, the coincidence in their arrival date noted but not questioned.

The mothers were all in a flutter as they began to prepare for their next foray – Cassandra and Devon's wedding.

Hope didn't see Anthony for the rest of the day, and even at dinner, she did her best not to speak, allowing Faith to answer questions about their journey and their visit, for Hope had nothing to say about it, having not actually been there herself.

She did pay attention when her father began to ask Anthony about the progress he had made during his visit.

"My friend was actually able to help significantly," he said. "I believe we have broken the code and solved the next clue."

"You were able to do so without my book?" her father asked, fixing an eye upon him, and Hope felt a churning in her belly as she wondered if her father knew that Anthony had taken it.

"I shall have to review it tomorrow," Anthony replied without a change in his expression.

"How about tonight?"

"I am rather tired from the journey, if you don't mind," Anthony said. "I do not travel well."

Hope hid her smile. He didn't – although she had certainly found a way to keep his mind off his stomach over the bouncing roads.

He glanced at her quickly, his face reddening as he turned his eyes away hurriedly, obviously understanding what she was thinking.

So she was the one affecting *him* now. That was interesting. Very interesting indeed.

ANTHONY HAD BEEN AWAKE LATE into the night, replacing the book into its binding. He had been as quiet as possible as he had opened the desk, retrieved the cover, and then replaced the inside pages before returning the book. He was sure that he had gone unnoticed, and fortunately, when he met up with Lord Embury the next morning, the earl did not seem to hold any suspicions as they opened the desk together.

They lay the books out on his work table in the library, and as they took a seat, Anthony explained Reeves' theory. Lord Embury seemed intrigued.

He agreed to give Anthony some time with the books, returning a few hours later to check on Anthony – who, of course, had already figured out the clue with Reeves, although he hadn't been able to admit it to Embury.

"A song?" Lord Embury said, his bushy eyebrows rising, and Anthony hesitated. He wasn't sure that it was for him to share the broken code with anyone – even Hope's father – but he also didn't see the harm. If he had no idea what he was supposed to do with the next clue, how would Lord Embury?

"A Spanish song," Lord Embury mused, rubbing his chin. "It could be tied to Ashford's grandmother – she came from Spain to marry the duke."

"Perhaps Covington will have an idea, then," Anthony said, wondering what Gideon would make of it all.

"Perhaps. We make for Castleton in a few days," the earl said, pausing as he sat back in his chair to stare at Anthony. "What will you do after the wedding?"

Anthony rubbed his chin, as he wasn't entirely certain himself. There was what he *should* do – and then what he wanted to do. "I suppose I will return home," he said slowly. "I have been remiss from my duties."

"Your mother is welcome to stay on here at Newfield when you return," the earl said. "She has certainly kept my wife occupied, for which I am grateful."

"There is something else," Anthony found himself saying, surprising even himself. It shouldn't have anything to do with the earl, and yet he knew, deep down, why he cared what the man thought – because his approval could make a great difference in a potential future with Hope. One that he didn't allow in the foreground of his mind, for it seemed almost too good to be true.

"Yes?"

"When I was visiting with Reeves, we were discussing how to prove my father's innocence. We have some ideas, and I hope to show beyond any doubt that he was set up to make it look as though he was the one who was the traitor. I am beginning to believe that the man in question was, in actuality, providing him the codes."

"I see," the earl said, before pausing for a moment and then narrowing his eyes at him. "Which of my daughters are you after?"

"Pardon me?" Anthony said, sitting back in surprise.

"Just why are you trying to prove yourself to me?"

"I am trying to prove the *truth* – to everyone who knew my father," Anthony said, focusing on keeping his tone even as the earl's words rankled him.

"I have plans for both of my daughters," Lord Embury said, fixing him with a hard stare. "Plans that do not include you. Now, despite my better judgement, I have welcomed you into my home and allowed you access to one of my most prized possessions. To allow you to stay any longer, however, would have people talking. Do you understand?"

"I do," Anthony said coldly as he stood, hating himself and his lack of restraint. He had heard enough. Embury's feelings toward him reiterated everything he had told himself, including all of the reasons he should not have allowed things to go as far as they did with Hope.

He'd have to continue reminding himself that their coming together had been nothing more than a moment in time.

A moment that he would remember for the rest of his life.

CHAPTER 21

"*C*assandra, this is beautiful!"

Hope reached over and placed her hand on her friend's arm. They had just arrived at Castleton, Cassandra's home – at least for now. After the wedding, which was to take place in Castleton's chapel, Cassandra would leave for her new husband's estate.

Castleton's ballroom was covered in floral arrangements and draperies. Hope knew that Cassandra's family had fallen upon hard times since her father had become ill, afflicted with a disease of the mind, but her family had done all they could to make Castleton look its best for the wedding this week.

As it was, only their closest friends and family were in attendance, which Cassandra told Hope was what she had wanted, anyway.

Faith had not yet joined them downstairs, and they were still waiting on the remainder of the guests to arrive. Hope was pleased they had been one of the first, for it meant she had some time with Cassandra. Anthony had, of course, joined Cassandra's brother, Gideon, and her fiancé, Devon.

Even as she reminded herself that he had no reason to share his whereabouts with her, she couldn't help but wonder what he was doing right now.

"Hope, I must thank you," Cassandra said now, stopping in the entrance of the ballroom, turning to place both of her hands on Hope's arms.

"Whatever for?" Hope asked, perplexed.

"If you had not spoken to Devon when he was upset with me and told him the truth of my affections, then we would not be where we currently are today. I would not finally be marrying the man I was meant to be with. Thank you so much."

"Of course, although I'm sure you'd have figured it out eventually," Hope said, remembering the day she had sought out the man her friend had loved for years to try to help him to understand that Cassandra wanted nothing but his love. It had taken some courage, but she had known that she would never forgive herself if she didn't do what she could to help the two of them.

"Now, tell me about Lord Whitehall's presence in your home."

"He accompanied his mother on her visit," Hope said quickly, glancing around to ensure they were not overheard, although she didn't miss Cassandra's pointed look. "And, of course, he was there to study the books. We do have some exciting news, but we should wait until we are all together to discuss it."

"Oh, Hope, do not make me wait like that," Cassandra said, squeezing her arm in glee.

Hope smiled impishly, part of her simply glad that Cassandra didn't ask further questions about Anthony. "It will be worth it," she said. "I promise you that."

* * *

ANTHONY DID NOT ENJOY BEING the center of attention.

But that was exactly what he was as all eyes in the drawing room were currently firmly fixed upon him.

"So," Ashford said impatiently, "did you find anything?"

"I did," Anthony said, carefully avoiding Hope's eyes. For he should be saying 'we', but he couldn't very well admit Hope's involvement to the rest of the group, even though her sister knew the truth. "It took some time, and I had to consult with another codebreaker, the man who taught my father, but I did."

"You showed the books to someone else?" Ashford said, frowning.

Anthony straightened. "You all wanted the code broken. It is broken. And, as it happens, I trust this man with my life."

"My father also saw the books," Hope interjected. "We had to tell him, since he had one of them and was not willing to share it. He said that it was given to his ancestors by Cassandra's grandmother years ago."

"I see," Lord Ashford said, obviously still suspicious, while Lady Cassandra leaned forward eagerly.

"What did you find?" she asked.

"A song," Hope said, clasping her hands together in obvious excitement. Anthony shot her a look of warning and she stilled. "Er, a song is what Lord Whitehall discovered," she finished, sinking back into her chair.

"A song?" Cassandra said with a frown of confusion. "What kind of song?"

"A Spanish one," Anthony said. "Lady Hope seemed to recognize it."

"Can you sing it for us?" Cassandra asked, and Hope colored slightly, but nodded. Anthony knew that as shy as she could be, she was used to playing music for a crowd.

She began the lines, her voice warming him through, as he wished he could walk over to her and kiss her thoroughly.

He loved the sound of her voice, the way she took a breath of encouragement before beginning anything. He loved how she would send him these small smiles that told him she was thinking about him, that she saw beyond his gruff exterior to the man he was inside.

Hell, he— he loved *her*. As he watched her standing there at the front of the room, listened to the song flowing through her lips, she seemed to be touching every part of him, and he had to fight the instinct to walk over to her and tell her exactly what he was feeling.

But then he heard Lord Embury's voice in his head, and he knew that not only could he not show his desire for her now, but to continue to do so even when they were alone would only bring censure upon his head. He was going to be broken by having to leave her. All he could do now was ensure that he didn't make this any harder for her than it already would be.

He had thought that if he could prove his father's innocence, he could approach Lord Embury to discuss a potential future with Hope. It was hard to imagine, after all of these years, that he would consider marriage, but he had also come to realize that the thought of Hope with anyone else was nearly more than he could bear.

But it didn't appear that he had any choice in the matter.

"What do you think it means?" Cassandra asked once Hope had finished, and Anthony was drawn out of his stupor to respond when he realized that she was addressing him.

"I have no idea," he said with a shrug. "I may have some experience with codes, but as for the song... it could be another riddle, I suppose."

"Does anyone speak Spanish?" Hope asked, seeming to shrink back when all eyes of the nine other people in the room turned toward her. "Does it make any sense?"

"Both Cassandra and I do, being that it is a language of

our ancestors," Ashford said, his brows drawing upward as he considered the words. "But nothing comes to mind."

"Perhaps we could play it in front of my parents as well as your own?" Lady Cassandra asked. "We do not have to tell them the reason for it, but it might resonate with one of them."

"We should have a chance tomorrow," her brother said, and Cassandra sat back down, deflated.

"That seems so long away. But very well."

"Hope, will you be the one to play it?" Lady Cassandra asked. "You are by far the most proficient musician out of all of us."

"Of course," Hope murmured, dipping her head. "I believe Lord Whitehall is also rather talented."

Now it was Anthony's turn to receive the scrutiny, which he understood. He hadn't shared with any of them his own ability to play. It had been another skill taught by his father, and one that always saddened him, for it made him think of him and all that he had lost in his death.

"I am nothing compared to Lady Hope," he said, staring at her as he said it, needing her to understand the truth to his words – which he meant in far more than simply music. "We shall listen to her."

* * *

HOPE PAUSED with her hand on the door handle. She knew that she should stay in her room, that she was risking everything by tiptoeing down the hallway in the middle of the night.

But she couldn't help herself. With so many people in residence at Castleton, it was unlikely that she was going to find any other opportunity to speak with Anthony alone. He had all but ignored her for the entirety of the day, refusing to even look at her or give her the chance to catch his eye. She had seen him walk into his bedroom earlier, which was in a separate corridor from hers but close to the top of the stairs.

It had given her an idea, one that was very daring but that she couldn't stop herself from acting out.

What he would think, she had no idea, but she had to speak to him. The not knowing was tearing her apart.

She knocked softly on the door, hoping that no one else nearby would hear her.

He answered quickly, his eyes widening in surprise when he saw her standing there.

"Hope," he said, looking behind her to make sure that no one saw her before pulling her in quickly. "What are you doing?"

"I had to see you," she said, wringing her hands together as her nerves began to overcome her. "We haven't spoken alone since we met Faith at the inn."

"No," he said, his expression guarded. "I thought it would be for the best."

"Why?" she asked, looking at him imploringly. It was the question that had been on her mind for days now. "Since we returned from visiting Reeves, you seemed to have cut me off. Did I do something wrong? Was I too... too forward?" She hated that her voice squeaked at the end of the sentence.

"No," he said, turning and walking over to take a chair in front of the fireplace. "I just thought it was for the best."

She had to tell her legs to move as she walked over to sit in the chair across from him. "Why?"

He paused for a moment, staring into the flames. "I told you that you and I could not be together."

Hope took a breath. This was what she had wanted to discuss. "I know you said that. But I thought that, just maybe..." How was she supposed to say this? "You felt something more for me."

He turned to her now, and the turmoil in his eyes nearly took her breath away. "Does it matter if I do?"

"Yes!" she exclaimed. "Of course it does."

"Your father does not want us to be together," he said. "Nor your sister. Cannot say I have asked your mother's opinion, although I'm sure she would be happy to offer it."

She gripped the edges of her chair. "Does it bother you?"

"What your family thinks?" He said, his voice harsh, his fingers gripping the edge of his chair. When he looked at her, his face was tight in frustration. "Yes, Hope. It does. What did you think we were going to do, run away to Gretna Green?"

Hope recoiled slightly, feeling the sting of his words. "I..." She looked away from him, toward the side of the room, trying to will away the tears that threatened to form. "I just..." she tried again, but then, before she knew what was happening, his arms were around her, scooping her up and out of the chair, holding her close.

"I'm sorry," he said, snuggling his nose into the crook of her neck, his arms tightening around her. "I'm sorry, Hope, for everything." He sat back in his chair, holding her flush against him. "This is all my fault. I never should have let it get this far, knowing that it couldn't be, but I couldn't help myself. For everything about you leaves me wanting more. I don't know what you see in me, but the last thing I want to do is to hurt you."

"Then don't," she said in a whisper, staring up at him, stroking the side of his cheek. "Does it really matter what everyone else thinks? If you feel for me what I do for you, then how could we ever be with any other?"

"I don't ever want to think of you with another man," he growled, holding her tighter, and she leaned back to gaze at him in supplication.

"Then be with me. In truth. Not for a moment, not for a week, but for a lifetime."

He didn't answer her with words, and as his lips crashed down upon hers, for a moment, she wondered if this was his way of not disappointing her, but she forgot her worries as he made love to her mouth with the same passion he had to her body before. Still holding her in his arms, he stood and walked her over to the bed, laying her down gently on top of it.

She felt like the most treasured of women as he slowly, gently, unfastened her nightgown and slid it down her arms, his lips trailing kisses on the skin he bared to the air. Hope kept her half-closed eyes upon his face, noting the tenderness in his gaze as he looked down upon her.

No matter what he said, she knew he cared for her, could feel it in the way he lovingly caressed her, the way his tongue teased each of her nipples, the way he so carefully put her nightgown to the side, as though to ensure it wouldn't wrinkle.

There was also the fact that every time they had made love, he had always first made sure that she was content, ready, and completely fulfilled and enjoying what he was doing to her. Even now, his fingers were at that sensitive place between her legs, gently massaging it as she opened her thighs up to him, inviting him in.

He unfastened his trousers, his eyes meeting hers with question in them, and when she pulled him close, he groaned into her mouth as his lips met hers again, his tongue moving in time with his hips as he thrust into her.

He began slowly, languidly, lovingly, but as Hope began to move more urgently beneath him, he answered in kind, and as they rocked against one another, Hope had to press her mouth against his shoulder in order to stifle herself from calling out his name.

When the colorful wave washed over her, she bit into his skin, even as she whimpered "Anthony," and he groaned her name into her ear in his own response as he lifted from her for a moment to finish beside her.

Afterward, she curled up against him, her head on his chest, and he stroked her back, raining kisses on her hair.

In that moment, she knew that it didn't matter what her father or her sister said, or whether or not he ever cleared his family name.

She was his, and he was hers.

Nothing else mattered.

CHAPTER 22

"What has you so aggravated this morning?"

Anthony arched an eyebrow at Lord Ferrington. The elder of the Rowley brothers scoffed at his own question.

"I should add, more so than usual."

"I'm fine," Anthony growled back. All of the men were scattered around the terrace in the gardens, waiting for the ladies to join them to walk to Castleton's small chapel.

The wedding was taking place this morning, and then he would be free to leave. Away from Hope. But even if she wasn't with him in person, he knew that she would never leave his thoughts, would be present with him for the rest of the days.

When she had come to him last night, he never should have let her in the door. But how could he have turned her away? The moment he had said the words that he knew had hurt her, something inside of him broke, and he hadn't been able to stop himself from doing everything he could to make it all better.

Which had led to the very thing that they had both wanted, but that he had told himself to no longer allow.

"Does your extra surliness have to do with a certain Lady Hope?" Ferrington asked, causing Anthony's head to turn to him so quickly he felt a twinge in his neck.

"Why would you think that?" he asked, before realizing that he was likely only implicating himself.

Ferrington grinned widely, leaning in closer. "I've seen the way you look at her. Not to worry. I won't say a thing to anyone."

"It doesn't matter anyway," Anthony said, crossing his arms and looking around the gardens, which were rather unkempt beneath the day that was as dreary as his mood. "Her father has all but forbidden us to be together."

"I see," Ferrington said, his usual cheerful face changing to a frown. "Because of the rumors surrounding your father?"

Anthony nodded. "Apparently. Although I've told Embury that I can prove my father's innocence and he told me that he hoped it wasn't on account of interest in one of his daughters, for he apparently has other plans for them."

Ferrington rubbed his brow. "I'm sorry to hear that." He paused. "How are you hoping to clear your father's name?"

Anthony sighed. He didn't have many close friends, and he supposed that Ferrington was as good as any. He also seemed genuinely concerned, so he didn't see the harm in sharing with him.

"When he was breaking codes that were intercepted by the French, he was given the codes by a lieutenant in the army. One who is now retired," he said. "I was hoping to pay him a visit the next time I was in London."

"The lieutenant being...?"

"Lieutenant George Johnson."

Ferrington's brow lifted, and his eyes lit up. "I believe I can be of some help."

"You can?" Anthony said in some disbelief. Surely Ferrington must be jesting, although Anthony didn't find it at all amusing. "How?"

"My father knew him. He never had anything particularly good to say about him."

Anthony could only stare at him. Could this be true? Was this what he had been missing? Information from another source? If only he had spoken up earlier.

"Did your father ever say anything that would have led you to believe that the lieutenant was capable of being a traitor?"

Ferrington scratched his cheek. "I wish I had paid more attention, but I only remember passing conversations. I wasn't particularly interested in the topic. We should ask my mother later today."

"How am I to speak to your mother?" Anthony asked. He couldn't even remember what the woman looked like.

"I'll introduce you. Perhaps bring Lady Hope into the conversation to soften things, if you do not mind her presence for it. I'm assuming she knows as much as I do now?"

Ferrington was right. She had been involved in everything else up until this point. Anthony didn't see why it would matter if she learned even more about him.

"Very well," he said as the library terrace doors opened and women in all shades of pastels descended the stairs. There was only one he was interested in, however – the vision in blue who was practically floating down toward him, her smile wide, tendrils of her blond hair peeking out from beneath her bonnet. Then he caught sight of her father behind her, and Anthony's small smile faded altogether. For even if Ferrington was able to help, it didn't matter.

Not anymore.

* * *

CASSANDRA AND DEVON'S wedding was absolutely beautiful. Hope had to wipe away a few tears at the way in which they stared at one another so lovingly. All that they said to one another, all of the wishes they had for a life together echoed those that Hope envisioned for herself – and now there was a face on the man standing at the altar with her in her dreams. And his face was Anthony's.

She stole a glance at him now across the chapel, saw him look back over to her, but it wasn't loving tenderness that filled his expression. Instead, his jaw was tight, his brow pinched, and she wondered just what was causing him such discord.

She discovered the reason during the wedding breakfast afterward. The dining room table had been extended to seat them all, the glass chandelier reflecting sunlight so that it danced around the room. The table had been covered in white, while a rainbow of flowers that Hope recognized from the garden were spread over top of it. They had now finished their meal but were all taking their time rising from the table to move to the drawing room. There were so many of them that small conversations were taking place, scattered between one room and the other.

"Lady Hope, would you accompany me for a moment?" Anthony asked, and she nodded, surprised when they were joined by Lord Ferrington and his mother in a corner of the dining room, which had quieted as others had moved on to the next room.

"Mother, you know Lady Hope?" Lord Ferrington asked.

"Of course, dear," she said with a warm smile. Hope didn't know her well, but her impressions were that she was a kind woman. "It was such a beautiful wedding, was it not?"

"Very much so," Hope responded, although she was

distracted by Anthony, who seemed to be trying to silently communicate something to Lord Ferrington.

"Mother," Lord Ferrington began, "we wanted to ask you about Lieutenant George Johnson."

The countess' pleasant expression fell. "Now just why would you want to know about him? Your father couldn't stand the man." She looked around at the three of them. "My apologies if he is an acquaintance of yours."

"My father knew him as well," Anthony said, leaning in slightly. "My father was a codebreaker and Lieutenant Johnson was the man who coordinated with him, until my father was labelled a traitor."

"Was he working with Lieutenant Johnson and the French?" Lady Ferrington asked, surprising Hope. She wondered why she had been asked to be present for this conversation, but now she was too intrigued to ask for fear she would be asked to leave before all was revealed.

"My father was no traitor," Anthony said fiercely. "But I would like to know why you think Johnson was."

"Because my husband told me so," Lady Ferrington said. "He had proof, but he died before he could do anything with it."

It was Lord Ferrington's turn to look shocked, as his mouth dropped open. "Why did you not tell me about this?"

His mother shrugged. "I assumed that if your father had wanted you to pursue it, he'd have asked you to or left you instructions," she said. "I thought that perhaps he didn't want to put you in any danger."

"I'll take on the danger," Anthony said. "What is it that he knew?"

"He said that he had seen Johnson exchanging information with the French, and that he had documents proving it. They are back at Hollingworth, as far as I am aware."

Lord Ferrington turned to Anthony. "I will look straight-away, as soon as I return."

"Thank you," Anthony said. "I would certainly appreciate anything you can do. Thank you, Lady Ferrington. Thank you very much."

As Lady Ferrington walked away, he turned to Hope, obviously so excited that he had forgotten others were watching them.

"Did you hear that, Hope? This is exactly what I need."

Her heart lifted, for even though she wanted this for Anthony and his mother, she also couldn't help her selfish wish that it could mean a future for the two of them, one that even her father couldn't deny.

The glimmer of hope for her happy ending was in sight. She just had to make sure nothing prevented it.

"That is good news," she said, smiling up at him. "In the meantime, what do you plan to do?"

"Well," he said, running his hand through his hair. "We can continue to try to solve the riddle of this song, although I'm not sure what else I should have to do with it. It's Gideon's treasure to find, and my role was to break the code. Which I did. Gideon asked if I could look over the books one more time to see if I missed anything, but I don't see how that could be."

"Do you have the books here?" Hope asked.

"I do," Anthony said. "Your father agreed that I could bring them, as he would be here to ensure that all was well. Of course, he will want to be present if we are to inspect them. I'm not entirely certain how Ashford will feel about that."

"I'm sure he will understand."

"It is a mystery, isn't it, how your father came to be in possession of the book?" he mused. "His mother must have been great friends with Ashford's grandmother."

Hope saw his gaze catch something over her shoulder – something that must have troubled him, for his expression became completely closed off.

"We should continue on to see the others," he said, all levity removed from his voice.

Her heart fell. She was enjoying this time alone with him and wasn't sure there would be much more. "But—"

"Hope."

Her father was behind her, and she turned to find him staring at her and Anthony, a frown on his face. "Go find your friends."

She bristled at his command. "Anth—Lord Whitehall and I were just about to do so."

"I would like to have a word with him first."

"Father, I—"

"Go, Hope."

She looked at Anthony, who nodded slightly at her as though to say he would be just fine, before she turned and went to find Cassandra.

She could only imagine what her father might have to say. And she had a feeling it wasn't anything good.

CHAPTER 23

"*L*ord Whitehall, I have asked you this before and I must ask you again."

Anthony braced himself for the earl's next words, which were more predictable than the sunrise.

"What are your intentions—"

"Whitehall, there you are!"

Anthony had never been so grateful to see Ferrington in his life. "We have been looking for you. Lord Embury," Ferrington continued. "Didn't see you there. A beautiful day for a beautiful ceremony, is it not?"

Lord Embury grunted in response.

"Ashford is looking for you," Ferrington continued, speaking to Anthony now. "He'd like to look at the books this afternoon, before anyone leaves."

Suddenly, Anthony wasn't so happy to see Ferrington, for he hadn't wanted to discuss this in front of Embury any longer.

"Tell me when you are doing so," Embury said with a pointed look at Anthony that also told him he likely wasn't finished with their previous discussion. "I will join you."

Anthony had known he would be spending some time trying to solve this riddle while at Castleton, but he hadn't planned on doing so much of it with Embury looking over his shoulder.

"He said later this afternoon," Ferrington said. "But first, we will go toast the happy couple once more."

Anthony was quick to walk away with Ferrington, leaving Embury behind them.

He wished the morning would last much longer, but it wasn't long before he was requested to appear in the library with Ashford.

Anthony had just entered his bedchamber to collect the books before their arranged meeting time when a soft knock on the door was followed by Hope's entry.

"What are you doing here?" he asked in a hushed voice. "Your father has warned me away from you yet again. I'm not sure that this is the best idea."

"I know," she said, taking a seat on the end of the bed. "But perhaps it is best that we are found alone. Then my father would have no choice but to allow us to be together."

Anthony raked a hand through his hair. "We'll have to discuss this later, for I am due to meet with your father in a few minutes."

"What are you discussing?" she asked, her eyes wide and bright, and he knew what she was hoping – that he was declaring his intentions for her. But doing so, especially now, would only drive them further apart.

"We are to look at the books," he said. "Ashford wanted to see them again, to determine if anything else within might help us with this new riddle. I doubt it, but I shall humor him. Your father wanted to be present, due to his increasingly failing trust in me."

"I see," she said, and he opened up the small bag he had carried the books in.

"What in the…" he muttered, placing the empty bag back down before quickly crossing to the wardrobe. He opened it, rifling through its contents, but all he could see within was his own clothing.

"Anthony?" Hope said from behind him. "Is something wrong?"

"Yes," was all he said, too intent on his current mission. He moved through the room as quickly as possible, opening every drawer, looking in every crevice, under the bed, behind all of the furniture. Nothing.

"Bloody hell," he muttered, forgetting Hope was there, and when she placed her hand on his back, he jumped, startled.

"I'm sorry," she said softly. "Perhaps if you tell me what is wrong, I can help?"

"The books," he said, both hands now in his hair as he looked around the room. "They're gone."

"What do you mean, they're gone?" she asked, her eyes widening.

Anthony had to take a breath. He didn't have time to explain, but he also couldn't brush her aside. "The books are always in my small bag. The same one I used when traveling to see Reeves. I put them in there when your father and I retrieved them before we left for the wedding and haven't removed them since. They're not there. Nor anywhere in the room."

Her eyes widened, her mouth forming an O.

"Could your valet have done something with them?"

"If he had, they would be somewhere in this room," Anthony said, beginning to pace back and forth.

"Did anyone else know they were here?"

"Yes, everyone knew. I'm to see Ashford and your father in minutes. I'll have to tell them that they are gone." His stomach churned at the thought.

"I'm sure it is nothing to be concerned about," Hope said, her optimism grating on Anthony's nerves. "We've already found the clue, have we not?"

"That is not the point," he said from between gritted teeth. "I promised your father that I would keep them safe. If I've lost the book he so prizes, how would he ever believe that I could—"

"That you could what?"

"That I could keep *you* safe?"

His words hung in the air between them, the only noise the inhale and exhale of her breath.

"You want to – be responsible for me, that is?" she said, and Anthony fought the urge to take her in his arms, inhale the fresh scent of her, take the strength he knew she would offer.

"It doesn't matter," he said, brushing by her instead. "I do not have that choice."

And without another look behind him, he walked out the door, leaving her – and her question – behind.

* * *

HOPE KNEW she should return to her friends, that to accompany Anthony would likely only cause further discord. But she couldn't stop herself from following him to see how this would all play out.

After Anthony brushed by her from the room, down the stairs toward the library, Hope waited but a few moments before taking the same path, trying not to rush so that Anthony wouldn't see her.

She had just reached the bottom of the stairs when Faith came upon her.

"I was looking for you," Faith said without preamble, and Hope tried to determine how she could quickly extricate herself from the conversation. This was going to be bad enough as it was – she didn't need Faith as a witness.

"You *what?*"

Their father's roar from the library could be heard from where they currently stood down the hall. Faith's head whipped toward Hope. "What is happening?"

But Hope didn't have time to explain. She hurried down the corridor, Faith following behind her. She only hoped that her father's reaction wouldn't bring the rest of the guests along with them. They didn't need such a large audience to witness her father's fury nor the wrath he was sure to bring down upon Anthony.

"His book is gone," Hope said over her shoulder when Faith wouldn't stop poking her finger into her shoulder, of course having no problem keeping up to her due to the length of her legs.

"What do you mean *gone*? Which book? *The* book?"

"Yes," Hope said, coming to a halt in front of the library door so abruptly that Faith ran into the back of her and almost knocked her over.

Lord Ashford was pacing back and forth across the floor of the library, arms crossed over his chest, while their father's face was red in fury, and Anthony stood with his hands on his hips, clearly refusing to be cowed.

"Where did they go?" her father continued, and Anthony lifted his arms to each side.

"I wish I knew," he said, his voice much quieter, but steely, telling Hope that he was teetering on the edge of his temper. "They were in my bag since we left Newfield Manor. I went to retrieve them from my room, and they were both gone."

"I cannot believe that you lost them. Not after I entrusted you with them." Hope's father stepped closer toward Anthony, who stood tall, unmoving. "Unless you lost them on purpose."

"What is that supposed to mean?"

"It *means* that you are no different from your father. A man who turned on those who believed in him."

"Now, Lord Embury," Lord Ashford interjected. "That is hardly fair."

Anthony stepped closer now, getting into Hope's father's face. "My father was no traitor. And I would never do anything to jeopardize this for Ashford. Besides, what could I possibly gain from stealing books I was already in possession of?"

"Perhaps you gave them to someone else."

Anthony brought his thumb and index finger to the bridge of his nose, pressing against it, obviously trying to control himself.

"I have had enough of this conversation. I will speak to my valet. Perhaps he will have an idea. Ashford, could you ask your servants to look for them as well?"

"Of course," Lord Ashford said. "I know we already solved the clue, so that is not my concern so much as *why* someone would take them. Combine this with the fact that Cassandra and Lord Covington were shot at—"

"What?" Lord Embury burst out. "No one ever told me that there could be danger involving this damned riddle."

He glared at Anthony as if it was his fault.

"I told you not to go with him," Faith hissed in her ear, and Hope elbowed her, but it was too late. They were noticed in the doorway.

"This doesn't concern you," their father said when he saw them. "Continue on and I will be with you shortly. We should be leaving soon."

"We are all involved in this, Father," Hope said, but it wasn't the right tactic, for her father's face only reddened.

"I want you as far from this as possible," he said. "If I had realized that Lord Whitehall was bringing danger to my household…"

"Father," Hope attempted, but he was already shaking his head.

"Out. And no more conversations with this traitor."

Anthony's jaw set, his hands curling into fists.

"I have tried to prove myself to you, but at what end, I have no idea," Anthony said. "Good luck with your search, Ashford. I'm done with it. With all of this."

He looked at Hope, his eyes hard and unrelenting. Her stomach churned as she understood what that look was saying, without any words accompanying it. He was done with her family, done with her, refusing to fight for the two of them and what she knew they had.

"Don't go," she said, her words so soft that she wasn't sure anyone would be able to hear her, but she hoped that Anthony could understand what she was trying to say, would read into her truest wish.

"I must," he muttered, as he walked by her and to the door. She reached out, grasping his elbow, no longer caring about who might be watching them or what they might think.

"Please?" she whispered, looking at him, clutching his arm.

"What is this about?" her father interjected, his stare upon them obvious, but Hope no longer cared about what was expected of her, what would make everyone else happy. She refused to remove her gaze from Anthony, intent on him and him alone.

If he gave her any indication that he would commit himself to her, she would leave her father and turn her back on any warnings he might issue.

"Hope?" her father said, but she didn't turn around, keeping her eyes firm on Anthony.

"Is there something going on here?" her father said, his bluster growing. "Hope Newfield, if you have an idea of tying yourself to this man, think again. I will not have our family name attached to theirs."

"That is not for you to decide, Father," she said, her heart tripping over the courage it took her to say such a thing. Anthony's eyes widened slightly in surprise, and she waited for him to agree, to tell her that she was right, to take her in his arms – to do anything besides stand there, frozen in indecision.

"That is where you're wrong," her father continued, oblivious to her silent plea. "For while I may not be able to stop you from giving up your life to be with him, I will make sure that neither of you ever receives anything from your dowry and you will not be welcome in my home ever again. Do you understand me?"

Hope's breath caught, as she finally turned to face him. "You would truly do that to me?"

"You would only be doing it to yourself," he said coldly. "The choice is yours."

Tears welled up in Hope's eyes, but if that was the way her father was going to be, then he had made the decision for her. She turned to tell Anthony, but as she did, the library door slammed behind them so hard that she heard the keys of the piano in the adjoining room jingle.

He was gone – without giving her any chance at all.

CHAPTER 24

"*W*here are you going?"

Hope had wrenched open the library door, following Anthony out, but Faith was close behind her, tugging at her arm as she questioned her.

"To speak to Anthony."

"Why?"

"To tell him how I feel."

"Hope." She tugged so hard now that Hope had no choice but to whirl around and face her.

"What is it?"

"You cannot seriously be considering a future with him. Did you not hear all that Father just said?"

"Of course I did," Hope responded incredulously. "That is the very *reason* I am making my choice. If Father is going to give me such an ultimatum, then he has made the decision easy for me."

"But do you have an option with Lord Whitehall? He didn't even stay to support you."

"Yes, but—" Hope stopped. Faith was right. Why had he not stayed? Her father may have rejected him, but she certainly hadn't. In fact, she thought she had made it obvious what she had wanted.

"Has he ever given you any inkling that he wants a future with you?"

Hope bit her lip. "He has said he cares for me."

"That is not the same thing."

Lifting her chin, Hope took a breath. "I believe that he thinks he has nothing to offer me until he proves that his father is innocent of the accusations against him," she said. "Perhaps after that…"

"What if that never happens?" Faith persisted. "I'm sorry, Hope. I do not wish to be the one to point this out to you, but you need to be logical about this before you give up everything for a man who might not actually want you."

The tears surfaced again, pricking the backs of Hope's eyes. She hated all that her sister was saying, yet, deep within, she knew that Faith had a point.

"There is only one way to know," she said resolutely. "I must ask him."

"Well, you cannot go up to his bedchamber alone," Faith said, narrowing her eyes. "At least, not now in the light of day when everyone will know where you have gone."

She was right, of course. There were far too many guests and servants about. It was not like he would leave immediately, not without his mother. Hope would find her and wait for him to come and tell her if he decided to leave. Then she would ask him for a moment to speak to him alone.

She followed Faith through the halls to the drawing room where some of the ladies were taking tea together. She made her greetings without any enthusiasm, sitting on the sofa, across from the piano in the corner. She stared at it, remembering Anthony slamming the door, the shock of the striking keys from between the walls.

The more she stared at it, the more she felt a tug on her

mind, telling her she was missing something. But what? It was too hard to concentrate with all of her worries about Anthony at the forefront of her thoughts.

She knew how much she wanted a future with him and only him – but was Faith right? Did he still want to live his life alone?

"Hope? Are you all right?"

Hope was pulled from her daze to find Percy sitting next to her, concern on her face.

"I-I'm not sure," she answered truthfully.

"Does this have to do with Lord Whitehall?" Percy asked in a low voice.

"How did you know?" Hope asked, her eyes flitting over to Faith, wondering if she had said anything.

"This did not come from Faith," Percy said with a quirk of her lips. "I have seen the way you look at him – and the way he looks at you."

"How does he look at me?" Hope couldn't help but ask, not caring that she was giving her true feelings away.

"Like he loves you," Percy said, tilting her head with a smile.

"I don't believe that's true," Hope said, her voice rather mournful.

"I do not believe Lord Whitehall is one who knows how to share his emotions very well," Percy mused. "I heard the disagreement in the library earlier – most of us did, if the truth be told," she said when Hope cringed. "All I can say, Hope, is that you deserve to be happy – whether that is with Lord Whitehall or without him. And so does he. None of us should have to suffer for the sins of our parents."

"This is true," Hope said, her eyes wide as she looked at her friend. "But how do I convince him of this as well?"

"I'm not sure that you can," Percy said gently. "It might be something that he needs to discover for himself. But perhaps your belief in him – and in the two of you – could let him know that it's possible."

"Perhaps," Hope said, comparing Percy's words to Faith's. The problem was, she didn't have the words from the one person who mattered – Anthony himself.

When the tea was over, she finally did what she had been waiting to do for hours – she snuck up to his room to talk to him. If he wasn't there, she determined, she would wait for him until he returned.

She pushed open the door without knocking, belatedly realizing that his valet could be within, but stepped through anyway.

Only to find that the room was not only devoid of Anthony himself, but all of his belongings as well.

He was gone. Without even so much as a goodbye.

Anthony was miserable.

He had departed Castleton as soon as he and his valet had been able to pack his belongings, before he had even spoken to his mother.

He had left her a note instead but had left nothing for Hope.

He was aware that he had taken the coward's way out.

He was no better than his father, who had also refused to stand up for himself and the truth.

But he knew that if he had stayed any longer, if he had spoken to Hope even one more time, he might have done something even worse. He might have promised her a future together, when her father had ensured that they would never have one.

For even if they had disregarded all that her father had said and run away to be married, he knew that Hope would never be truly happy. She might be happy for a time, but he knew how much her family meant to her, and he never wanted to subject her to the same rumors and whispers that he and his mother had endured for years.

He had done this *for* Hope, even though he knew that she would likely never forgive his betrayal. The way that she had been staring at him in that library, asking him by just the way she looked at him, to commit to her, to tell her that all was going to fine, to make everything better, had nearly broken him.

If she hadn't turned away from him for just that one moment, he would have been a man lost to her and whatever she asked of him.

But now he was a man lost to something else – to grieve over what could have been. A life with Hope.

* * *

THEY WERE PLANNING to leave Castleton the next morning. Hope had tried, during the past couple of days, to maintain a happy smile for Cassandra's sake. This was, after all, to be one of the joyous times of Cassandra's life.

But deep within, her heart was broken.

Anthony had left her as though all they had experienced together meant nothing. Perhaps everything he had said to her were just words, with no true meaning behind them, his actions but those of a man interested in a woman only because of her presence.

"Hope?" Faith opened the door after a short knock and entered her bedchamber. "Mother is nearly ready to leave."

Hope nodded, looking around her. Her bags were packed neatly by the doorway, her maid having taken care of most of it. She smiled sadly to herself as she thought of the last time she had traveled, when she had packed for herself. A journey she would remember forever for its simplicity and as the time when she had fallen in love with Anthony.

"Are you all right?" Faith asked, her brow furrowed in concern as she walked farther into the room.

"No," Hope said morosely, no longer hiding her feelings from her sister. "The truth is, Faith, I thought that Anthony and I had forged something together. I thought that he cared for me as I did him. But it seems I was wrong."

"Did you want him to stand up to Father?"

"I suppose I wanted him to not allow *anything* to come between us," Hope said. "Father or his family history or anything else that might have threatened how we felt for each other. Does he not realize that I don't care what was said about his father? That all that matters is how we feel?"

"Is that enough?" Faith asked with unusual gentleness. "For you, or for him?"

"It should be," Hope said, and Faith leaned over and placed her hand on Hope's.

"You are a woman who sees the world in color, who sees the best in everyone she meets, who loves without condition," she said. "You are the type of person that I need in my life. As does, I believe, Lord Whitehall."

"I thought you didn't want me to have anything to do with him."

"I didn't," Faith said before a self-deprecating smile crossed her face. "I have realized, however, that he and I are actually rather alike. We tend to plan for the worst that could come our way, look at things in fear of what may be. He likely left Castleton because he didn't want you to have to make a choice. Perhaps after Father's threats, he believed that if you chose him, you would come to regret it."

Hope tilted her head as she looked at her sister. "A wise thought, but I am not sure that is any better, for it means that he thinks he can make the decision for me."

"Because he already knew what you were going to choose," Faith said, pausing for a moment. "I am sorry, Hope, for judging him so quickly. I have never seen you as happy as when you were with him, and I shouldn't have listened to Father so readily without discovering the truth – or at least listening to Lord Whitehall's defence."

Hope rose and walked to the window, crossing her arms over her chest. "What now?"

"Now, you take back the power and make your decision – and tell him why you have made it. That is what would change my mind."

Hope nodded, turning around, back toward her sister. "A decision based on fact and not emotion."

"That's right."

"I might need some time to think on that."

"If I am right at what he feels for you, then you have time. He will not be finding another, that is for certain." Faith stood herself. "Well, I best go finish packing. It will not be long before we leave. I do feel for Lord Ashford, however. He had so much hope in solving this riddle, and it all came to nothing."

"We did discover a beautiful song," Hope said wistfully, a smile playing on her lips as she thought of it. "I never did play it. Once the books were stolen, all else was forgotten."

She stopped suddenly, the idea hitting her with the full force of a punch to the stomach.

"That's it!" she said excitedly, her hands nearly shaking in front of her.

"What's it?" Faith asked, as alert as Hope.

"The song. The piano. I think I've solved the puzzle."

CHAPTER 25

*H*ope hurried across the room, Faith following after her.

"Hope, what are you talking about?"

"The piano," she said, rushing down the staircase as fast as her kid slippers would allow her. When she reached the landing, she nearly broke out into a run toward the drawing room. "I thought there was something to it," she said, slightly panting with exertion now. "It's like the desk. Father's desk. It could be a puzzle. We must find Cassandra."

"I think she is in the front parlor, saying her farewells as people leave," Faith said, keeping up with Hope now. Hope veered off course from the drawing room to the parlor, stopping in the doorway, not caring any longer who might see her in such dishevelment.

"Cassandra!" she said, catching sight of her just as she was about to see off Madeline. "I have an idea. Come to the drawing room."

She turned and began down the corridor before Cassandra responded, although from the look of her open mouth she was certainly interested in what Hope had to show her.

"Hope," Faith said, not showing any effort whatsoever. "A word of caution – your idea is a sound one, but it could come to nothing. Perhaps we should have tested your theory before involving Cassandra." She looked behind them to see that more of their friends had joined in following them. "Or anyone else."

Hope had a feeling, however, deep in her stomach, that she was right. Her intuition was usually fairly accurate – except, it seemed, when it came to Anthony. But on this, she was certain.

"I'm right, Faith," she said, pulling out the bench and taking a seat at the piano. "I know I am."

She placed her fingers against the smooth, cool keys. She had played this instrument before, during many evenings that were spent in the drawing room, some with the gentlemen, some without. Sitting in front of any instrument was like coming home to her, and she lovingly stroked the keys before placing her fingers upon the correct ones.

She knew this was the answer. Anthony might have broken the code, but this part of the riddle was hers to complete.

She only wished that he was here with her. It wouldn't be the same without him.

Hope wasn't aware who all had followed them into the room, but it didn't matter as she was too focused on what she had to do next.

"*Mariana, mi amor, ha llenado mi corazón. Me ha dejado tan ligero y sintiendo calor,*" she sang, her fingers dancing over the keys. She had memorized the song, and she closed her eyes, playing the notes and singing the words from deep within her.

She was about halfway through when she felt the shift in

the piano, as though something moved within it. It was two bars later when she heard the *thunk*, and she slowed her playing as Cassandra and her brother rushed around to the back of the instrument.

"Well, I'll be," Lord Ashford murmured, as he reached into what seemed to be a new opening in the back of the piano and pulled out an item, lifting it up for all of them to see.

Hope looked around her now, finding that in addition to her, Faith, Cassandra, and Lord Ashford; Percy, Lord Covington, Lord Ferrington and Mr. Rowley had joined them.

"A key," Hope breathed, standing from the bench and leaning in. "For what?"

Lord Ashford turned to Cassandra, who shook her head. "I haven't seen anything like it."

Cassandra lifted her palm up to her brother, who placed the key within it.

"It has a ruby in the center," Cassandra murmured, looking at the small key. "There is also a small inscription." She peered closer at it. "It looks like it is in Spanish."

"Do these words make sense?" Lord Ashford asked, peering closer, reading. *"Una piedra preciosa, un regalo de amor, un destello de llama."*

"A precious stone, a gift of love, a flicker of flame..." Cassandra translated. "What could it be? Do you think it is in code?"

"I wish Whitehall was still here," Lord Ashford said with annoyance. "He was helpful in the past. Not only that, but if this has anything to do with the books, his memory is the next best thing to having them in our possession."

Hope wished he was still there as well, although for altogether different reasons.

"Eric and I will be heading his way, if he is at his estate,"

Mr. Rowley said. "Why do we not stop on our way home, to see if he can help?"

"You can send him the key itself," Lord Ashford said, surprising them all. "Not only do I trust him with it, but it seems that Castleton is not the safest place for anything regarding this riddle."

Hope sat back on the bench, pondering that. It was true, for it was here where Cassandra and Devon had been shot at, here where the books had been stolen.

"You think someone else at Castleton is after the riddle?" Cassandra asked, looking up at him in surprise. "How is that possible? We know and trust everyone here."

"I know," Lord Ashford said with a sigh of exasperation. "I don't know what to think anymore."

"Very well. We'll take the key," Mr. Rowley said. "We best get going so that we can reach him before dark. Then we can stay the night there."

They were all leaving the room, walking toward the front of the house when Hope had an idea. She chased after Mr. Rowley, tugging on his arm to stop him, drawing him into the shadows and speaking before she lost her nerve.

"I must ask a favor, if you don't mind," she said shyly. She hadn't spent a great deal of time with him before.

"Of course," he said with a nod. He had always been quite kind, and a studious man. Why couldn't she have fallen in love with a man like him instead? But no, it had to be Anthony.

"Would you… would you take a note to Lord Whitehall for me?" she asked. "It should take me but a moment to write it."

"We will be next after Lady Persephone and her family depart, so there is time," he said, and Hope hurried away, writing her note as quickly as she could while still ensuring it was legible before returning and passing it to Mr. Rowley, who folded it and tucked it into his pocket along with the key.

Then she took a breath, hoping that she had written the right words. The words that would make Anthony come back to her.

* * *

ANTHONY HAD BEEN LIVING in near darkness in his manor. His servants seemed to have been too nervous to come near unless it was necessary. Anthony had ridden his horse home and knew at some point he would have to make travel arrangements for his mother to return from Newfield Manor, but he would deal with that at a later time.

Which was why he was surprised when his butler announced that he had visitors that evening.

"Who?" he demanded.

"Lord Ferrington and Mr. Rowley, my lord," the butler said, before the two men appeared behind him, apparently not in the mood to wait for Anthony to be prepared to receive them.

"What are you doing here?" he asked, motioning for them to take a seat on the library furniture. He had a book open in front of him, although he had not actually been reading, but staring into the fire, wondering when it had all gone wrong.

"We come with a message," Lord Fitzgerald said before turning to his brother and sharing a grin. "Three in fact."

"Three messages," Anthony said, frowning at them, not in the mood for their games.

"Yes," said Mr. Rowley, reaching into his pocket. "First, the most intriguing."

He passed him a small object, which Anthony took with interest.

"A key," he mused.

"Yes, and not just any key," Mr. Rowley said. "It emerged from a piano at Castleton after Lady Hope played the song you deciphered."

Anthony's head snapped up at Hope's name, but he was also captivated by the context in which it was used.

"She played the song?"

"Yes. Apparently, she had the idea that perhaps the piano would work as a puzzle box, much like her father's desk."

"I should have thought of that," Anthony muttered, but Lord Ferrington shrugged.

"You're a codebreaker, not a clue master, are you not?"

"That's true," he said, still berating himself as he turned the key over in his hand, the gold smooth against his skin. He rubbed his thumb over the ruby. "Why did you bring this to me?"

"Ashford was hoping that you'd have an inkling of what the inscription meant. He thought perhaps the books might have held an idea. Since he no longer has the books, he figured your memory was the next best thing."

"Fair point," he said, biting his lip as he looked it over. "I will have to take some time to think on it."

"Very well. We will leave it with you when we depart – hopefully tomorrow. Do you mind if we stay here tonight?" Lord Ferrington asked.

"Of course. You are welcome," Anthony said, seeing his butler still hovering by the door and he asked him to bring his friends refreshments and prepare rooms for them. "I know I should allow you time to recover from travel, but now you have made me far too curious on what else you have for me."

"Message number two comes from our mother," Lord Ferrington continued.

"Your mother?"

"Yes. You recall what she said about Johnson."

"Of course."

"She had to return home before we did. It seems she found a few things in my father's old possessions. She sent a note as to what they included, and when we return to the estate, we will be happy to send them on to you, or to whoever might need to see them. They detail what Johnson was plotting and include a signed testimony from a French officer."

Anthony stared at him, aghast. "You cannot be serious."

"Oh, but we are," Lord Ferrington said, smiling triumphantly, although it was his brother who seemed far more regretful.

"We do apologize that we were not aware of this sooner," Rowley said. "We could likely have saved your family a great deal of hardship."

Anthony opened his mouth to agree, but then stopped. The brothers had gone out of their way to do this for him, had brought the message to him here when they could have returned home after a great deal of travel. He was fortunate that they had believed enough in him to search it out.

"Thank you," he finally said. "I do appreciate it."

"Does that change anything?" Lord Ferrington asked hopefully.

"About what?"

"Lady Hope."

Anthony's countenance fell. "I am not sure what you mean."

Lord Ferrington rolled his eyes. "You obviously have intentions for her. I assumed that with your father's name no longer muddied, you would make them known."

Anthony stood, walking across the library floor to stare out the window.

"Her father made it very apparent that even if my family's name is cleared, I am not a man for either of his daughters."

There was silence behind him, and he turned to find the brothers exchanging a look.

"Well," Mr. Rowley said, "she sent you a note. That is the third message."

He handed over a piece of paper, which Anthony pocketed, having no wish to read it in front of them.

"Thank you for bringing this – all of this – to me," he said. "How long will you be staying?"

"Just overnight. Then we will return home, as Noah here is off to Bath soon," Lord Ferrington said.

"Bath?" Anthony said in surprise. "What takes you there?"

"I am going to inquire into continuing my education," Mr. Rowley said. "I find living as a spare son does not quite fulfill my life's interests."

"Good for you," Anthony said, fighting the urge to leave the two of them to see just what Hope had written him. But perhaps this was best. He would do what was right and entertain his friends.

Then go back to feeling sorry for himself tomorrow.

CHAPTER 26

*A*s Anthony saw the Rowley brothers off the following morning, he could tell that they were curious as to what his note from Hope included.

It was not that he didn't want to share its contents with them.

It was that he hadn't yet read it himself.

As he had said goodnight to the men the night before, his first instinct had been to run to his room and open it up, to read whatever it was she had to say to him. But then he had stopped, wondering if doing so would change everything.

What if she had written that she never wanted to see him again? What if she had said she blamed him for everything, that she agreed with her father, that she had seen who he truly was after he had left without saying goodbye?

Even though it would be for the best if she had, he couldn't bring himself to open it and determine if he was correct.

So he left it, folded, on the table beside his bed.

Now he sat in his chamber, looking back and forth between the folded note and the key, which he held in one hand, turning it over and over as he read the inscription, trying to recall anything from the books that might be relevant.

"A precious stone, a gift of love, a flicker of flame. What could it be?" he murmured the words in English. "What could it *be?*"

He paced back and forth, wondering why nothing was coming to him, until it occurred to him that there was a block in his mind – and that block was Hope's note.

"Damn it," he said, finally pacing back over to the night-stand and picking up the note. He unfolded it slowly, annoyed that his fingers were practically shaking as he did so.

Anthony,

By now you will have received the key and, knowing you, have likely solved the inscription. I wish you had been here to accompany me. As I played the song to unlock the key, I knew it would have been so much better had you been here with me. I understand why you left, but know this. My heart is yours. It is now and always will be. It chose you, and it is up to you what to do with it now. I am yours if you will have me. The song unlocked the key, the key to my heart. I love you and always will.

I will be at Castleton for the next week before returning home.

Love always,

Hope

He let the note fall from his fingers to the floor. She loved him. He had known that she cared for him, as she of course would not have given herself to just any man, but to know that she was giving him every piece of her, no matter what her father said… it caused a great twinge in his chest, one that led to warmth spreading out to every part of his body.

That was love. He had known he loved her, but he hadn't understood how much his soul was entwined with hers, that, no matter what happened in the future, they would always belong together.

He had thought that staying apart was the right thing to do. When she had stood there, staring up at him, it had taken everything within him to push her away. But knowing he could prevent any ridicule, and also knowing that even if he hadn't been able to, she'd have given it all away anyway – any defenses that he originally had began to crumble down around his feet.

A small bit of hope began to creep in that perhaps – just perhaps – now that he could prove his family's innocence, her father would agree that he was the man for her – despite his insistence otherwise.

He looked down at the key now. The key to Hope's heart. The key to love.

The ruby embedded in the key shone back at him. A ruby. Love. Hearts. Could it be a necklace? Wasn't there a ruby jewellery set somewhere in the Sutcliffe family? Could the key have something to do with it?

There was only one way to find out. He had to return to Castleton – and to Hope. He only prayed she would still be there when he made it.

He called out to his butler to find his valet to pack for him, and to ready his horse. He had a journey to make.

ANTHONY WAS on the road within the hour. He hadn't taken much with him and had told his valet that he would either return soon or send for him so that he was unencumbered, but for the belongings packed into the saddlebags. He knew the way well, the road being rather straightforward. There was one shortcut he decided to take, however, once he neared Castleton.

Instead of staying on the road, he saw the opening in the path and cut across one of Ashford's fields. His eyes caught a flash in the trees beside him, but when he slowed his horse and turned to look, there was nothing but manicured hedge. He must be seeing things, especially now, when he was so close to Hope and insistent that nothing else must come between them.

As they came up to a hedgerow, he kicked his heels into his horse's side, urging Wildheart to jump up and over. His horse, well-trained, did so with grace, and when Anthony realized just how close he was to Hope, he began to urge his horse even faster.

He was nearing the next hedgerow when he heard the first shot. Wildheart reared back at the noise, not prepared for it. Anthony whipped his head around, trying to determine from where it was coming.

He should have used that time to concentrate on his horse, for when the second shot sounded, his horse was already nearing the next hedgerow, and the noise caused Wildheart to buck Anthony right out of his seat.

As Anthony felt the reins slip through his hands with nothing but air beneath him, all that he could think about was Hope.

Then everything went black.

* * *

"WHAT ARE YOU WAITING FOR?" Cassandra asked as she and Faith watched Hope pace back and forth before the parlor's front windows.

"I think the better question is *who* is she waiting for?" Faith said with a sly grin, and Hope fixed a look upon her.

"It's Lord Whitehall, isn't it?" Cassandra asked, Faith

already nodding before Hope could either confirm or deny it.

"I am only hoping that he soon returns with an answer to the clue," Hope said, but it was clear that she wasn't fooling anyone.

"He might just send a note," Faith said unhelpfully, and Cassandra stood, leaving her book on the table and placed her hands on Hope's arms.

"If he doesn't come here, then perhaps he is waiting until you return home," she said optimistically. "Maybe a change of scenery will help you as well."

Hope nodded, but she wasn't convinced. Anthony lived closer to Castleton than to Newfield. He was most likely to return here with the clue – unless he had seen her note and decided he would wait until she had departed so that he didn't have to see her.

"When do you leave?" Hope asked, changing the conversation.

"Tomorrow," Cassandra said. "Shortly before you."

"Of course," Hope said, annoyed at her own distracted-ness. "I knew that."

"Perhaps if you stop watching out the window, he might be more likely to appear," Faith said, not looking up from her book so she missed Hope's glare. But, as much as Hope hated to admit it, her sister was right. Watching and willing for him to arrive would not bring him to her.

"I am going to go play the pianoforte for a while," she said. "I will meet up with you again shortly."

She had just sat down at the piano in the drawing room and played a few bars – the Spanish clue again, a song that her fingers began playing before she even realized it – when the first shouts rang out. She stopped abruptly as she didn't recognize the voice echoing through Castleton's front foyer, and when she ran to the doorway and looked out, she was surprised to find a man she thought she recognized as the stablemaster standing there.

The butler hurried to the door, looking right and left as he tried to motion the stablemaster out the front door, but the man stubbornly remained where he was.

"Summon Lord Ashford," he said. "Wildheart has just appeared – alone."

"Wildheart?" the butler repeated, shaking his head as he obviously had no idea to what the man was referring. "Grimes, you best return outside. This is no place for—"

"Wildheart?" It was Lord Ashford who appeared this time, Lord Covington behind him. They must have been down in the billiards room. "Lord Whitehall's horse?"

A sick sense of dread began filling Hope's stomach.

"Aye," Grimes said with a grim nod. "The horse is uninjured, still wearing the saddlebag but appears agitated. No sign of Lord Whitehall."

Lord Ashford and Lord Covington exchanged a look before they practically sprinted down the corridor and out the door.

"What are you going to do?" Cassandra called after them as Hope remained frozen to the spot, her hand gripping the doorframe, unable to let go.

"We're going to find him!" Lord Covington called out behind him as they ran out the door.

All Hope wanted to do was follow them out and insist they take her with them, but she knew that she would only slow them down. She didn't realize that she was still standing there until she felt Faith's hand on her arm, and she slowly turned toward her.

"They'll find him," Faith said with more sympathy than she usually emoted. "Lord Whitehall is too stubborn to allow anything to happen to him."

Cassandra joined them and Hope turned to one of them

and then the other, finally forcing herself to move. "What do we do now?" she asked. "And do not say to wait. I have waited long enough."

"Why do we not walk around the gardens, perhaps down to the ruins?" Cassandra suggested. "He could have come that way. Who knows, maybe we will meet him as he walks up to the house."

The smile she forced on her face was not very believable, but Hope knew that Cassandra was doing this for her, so she simply nodded as they quickly changed into their boots and collected their bonnets before they left. Hope went through the motions woodenly, doing so out of practice instead of necessity – she would run through the woods barefoot if it meant finding Anthony.

They had made it as far as the ruins of the old house, walking in silence as they all knew that there was no point in saying anything, when they heard the first shout. They paused for a moment before, almost in unison, they picked up their skirts and broke into a run, following the sound.

When they crested the hill and saw what waited before them, they froze, a keening cry filling the air as below lay the man Hope loved, motionless on the ground behind the hedgerow. The scene was almost serene with the call of the birds, the sun shining down on the green grass below him. And yet there was something so impossibly wrong with it that Hope almost wondered if this was a nightmare she had wandered into, one from which she just could not wake.

It was the moment she decided he was dead when she realized that the cry was coming from her own mouth, and she lost all strength to stand as she collapsed into Faith's arms.

Utterly broken.

CHAPTER 27

*A*ll he could hear was music.

The song was a familiar one, one that tugged at his memories.

The Spanish one. About Mariana. It swirled round and round in his mind, the lyrics sung in that sweet, honeyed voice that belonged to the woman he loved more than any other.

Hope.

Where was he? Was he beyond this life and into the next? Had he done something right enough to allow him to listen to her sing for eternity? Or was this to be his torture, to hear her, so close, yet have her completely out of his reach?

But when he felt his chest rise and fall with a breath, he knew that, perhaps, he had been allowed to live another day.

Then the music abruptly ended and all that had happened came flooding back in remembrance. When his eyes flew open, even the dim light caused him to wince, his head pounding fiercely as he looked around the room.

He was at Castleton. Thank goodness. But how had he gotten here? And where was— He patted his chest, trying to find where he had placed the key, but it seemed that someone had changed him from his riding clothes.

He tried to sit up and push himself out of the bed, but there was too much pain when he did so, and he found he had no choice but to succumb and to lie back down again.

"Whitehall?"

He cracked his eye open again to find Ashford standing in his doorway.

"Are you alive, man? I was just passing your door when I thought I heard something from within. My God, it is good to see you awake."

Anthony opened his mouth to say something but found that it was far too dry to form sound. Ashford must have understood, for he found a cup of water beside the bed and helped lift it to his lips.

"We thought you were gone from this world for a moment."

"So did I," Anthony managed in a gravelly voice. "The key?"

It was all he could say at the moment, but Ashford must have understood, for he nodded. "We found it. Very clever, to hide it where you did."

Anthony managed a small smile. He had sewn it into his linen shirt, just above his heart. It had seemed appropriate.

"Good," he said.

"Do not worry about that now," Ashford said. "Once you are up and about, we can discuss it."

Anthony shook his head slightly, wincing in pain when he did. "Your family's rubies," he said. "I think that's what you need next."

Light of acknowledgment filled Ashford's eye at that, and he began nodding slightly. "Of course," he said, tapping his finger against his lips. "That makes sense. The first part of the riddle would be referring to a ruby, the second, a necklace. The jewels were my grandmother's, and, as far as I know, she brought them from Spain." He stood. "Before we get to that, however, I should find Lady Hope."

"Hope?" Anthony said, trying to slow the rapid beating within his chest at mention of her name. He wasn't sure that he was ready to see her. What was he to say?

"Of course," Ashford said, appearing slightly puzzled. "She has been sitting with you nearly every moment since we found you. She had left for but a few minutes when you awoke."

"Oh," he said stupidly, just as he noticed her figure in the doorway, her presence filling the room with light, lemon, and hope. Of course.

"I'll leave you for a moment," Ashford said, before one side of his lips quirked up. "Although if anyone asks, I never left you unchaperoned."

When he was gone, the room fell so silent that Anthony could practically hear the tension between them, a light buzzing that filled his ears. He wished that he wasn't in such a vulnerable state lying before her, that he could stand and take her in his arms and do what he yearned to do from the very center of him, which was to show her how much she meant to him, that he had been a fool for leaving her.

But instead he was lying here, unable to rise due to the pounding of his head. She entered the room tentatively, taking slow steps toward him as though she was scared.

"How are you feeling?" she asked in that soft, melodic voice of hers.

"I've been better," he said, not meaning for his tone to be as gruff as it was.

"I can imagine," she said, gracefully taking the chair beside the bed. She looked tired, not as vibrant as usual. "You had quite the fall."

He furrowed his brow. "All I can remember is the sound of shots. Wildheart—do you know how Wildheart is?"

"He's fine," she said with a small smile. "Actually, he was the one who alerted us to the fact that you were in trouble. He showed up at the stables with your saddlebag over his back but no rider."

"He's a good horse," Anthony said gruffly. He did love that horse. He reminded himself to bring him an extra treat the next time he saw him.

"That he is," she said, leaning forward with worry on her face. "Were the shots directed at you?"

"I have no idea," he said with a sigh, closing his eyes, "although the fact that Lord and Lady Covington were also shot at earlier this summer while similarly involved in this treasure hunt seems rather too much of a coincidence, does it not?"

"It does," Hope said. "Perhaps do not say anything to my father, as he is already worried enough."

Anthony groaned. "I can hardly believe that he has allowed you to remain here."

When all he was met with was silence, he opened his eyes to find Hope looking down at her clasped hands. He reached out and lifted her chin with his fingers, his heart dropping when he saw the tears in her eyes.

"Hope," he said in a low voice. "What is it?"

"I—" her voice broke. "I thought you were gone. Dead. That I would never have the chance to see you again. To touch you. To—" When she stopped and took a shuddering breath, Anthony wished with everything within him that he could take her into his arms and tell her that it was all going to be all right. But he couldn't. Because he didn't know that. "In that moment, when I saw you lying there, thinking you were d-dead, I knew one thing for certain. It didn't matter what my father said or wanted for me. A life without you is no life at all. Which I told him when we arrived back here and I realized that you were alive."

He kept his eyes on her, watching the expressions play out on her face.

"What did he have to say to that?"

"At first, he told me that I was being stubborn and a fool. But then—"

Anthony waited.

"Then my mother came into the room," she said, a slight smile playing over her lips. "She told my father that *he* was the fool, that if he continued to try to keep me from you, all that he was doing was pushing me away."

Anthony's jaw dropped open. "So he... he approved of your wishes, then?"

Hope cleared her throat. "'Approved' might be too strong of a word," she admitted. "But he no longer forbade a potential union."

She didn't meet his eye any longer, and he knew then the issue – he hadn't said anything about the note in which she had expressed all she felt for him. She had placed her heart out before him, and he hadn't responded.

"Why did you leave?" she asked, finally looking up at him, meeting his eye, and the hurt he saw within her face brought pain to his own chest.

He used his elbows to push himself up into a sitting position, ignoring the pain it caused his head.

"Anthony, don't—" she began, but he held up a hand to stave off her words.

"Hope," he said, reaching out and taking one of her hands in his. "I'm sorry. I truly am."

"You made me feel a fool," she said, her words harsher than he had heard from her before. "I have been the one telling you how I feel, giving you my heart, and you keep throwing it back at me. When I thought you had died, I knew how I felt, truly, but still, you have not allowed me in, and I—"

"Hope, I received your note," he interrupted her.

She sniffed softly. "Perhaps I was a fool to send it. You do not have to reciprocate my feelings, no matter what happened between us in the past. I just needed you to know—"

"Hope, I love you," he said, voicing the words aloud, causing fear to slice through his heart – fear at what it meant to say such a thing, for it could very likely change his entire world. And yet, the love had grown greater than the fear, and he could no longer contain it within.

Her gaze lifted to his, disbelief filling her eyes. "You do?"

"Of course I do. I think I have loved you nearly since the moment I met you."

"But then why—"

He sighed. "I was afraid of getting hurt again. And I was trying to protect you, to keep you from experiencing the ridicule that has followed Mother and me. I also didn't want to separate you from your family."

"What has changed?" she asked, which was a good question, for the truth was, even though he could now prove his father's innocence, that wasn't truly what had made the difference.

"I realized, as I sat at home in a lonely, empty house, reading your note, that nothing else in my life meant any more than you. That if I couldn't have you and your love, what else mattered? This code breaking and treasure hunting has been fun, but it was just an opportunity to spend time with you. Even if we never set foot in another *ton* event, what does it truly matter?"

"I feel the same," she said, tears spilling down her cheeks now. "All that I care is that we are together."

"And we will be," he said. "Once I can get myself out of this damn bed."

She laughed at that through her tears, although she was obviously trying to dampen her emotions, which he wished she wouldn't – not for his benefit.

"Come here," he said gruffly.

"I don't want to hurt you," she said. "The physician said that as long as you woke, your head would heal, although your ankle could pain you for the rest of your days. Fortunately, Lord Ashford knew a fairly gifted surgeon nearby."

"I'll be fine," he said. "I am rather stubborn. And even if I never fully heal, will you take a broken man?"

He was broken in more ways than just his ankle, but he knew that with Hope by his side, he could be whole in the ways that truly mattered.

"Always," she said, reaching up and running a hand over the stubble of his cheek.

At her promise, he leaned down and took her lips with his, pushing aside the pain in his head to focus instead on the pleasure of her mouth. She gave him all that she had – with gentleness – which he accepted with a great amount of appreciation.

When they finally broke apart and stared at one another with small smiles, he began to ask her a question but thought better of it.

"What is it?" she said, in tune with his emotions.

"I was going to ask you something," he murmured.

"But?"

"I should probably ask your father first."

"I see," she said, a smile dancing on her face. "What if he says no?"

He sighed. "Then I suppose I shall ask you anyway."

"Then do it now," she urged, and he studied her for a moment.

"Do you promise not to tell him that I asked you first?"

"Of course."

"Very well. Lady Hope Newfield," he said, taking a breath and tugging her in closer toward him. "Will you marry me?"

"I thought you would never ask," she said, before her smile grew to a full grin and she wrapped her arms around his neck.

He winced slightly but didn't care. She had agreed to be his, and that was all that truly mattered.

CHAPTER 28

"*C*an you hear anything?" Hope hissed, but Faith waved her hand away as she shushed her, leaning in so that her ear was flush against the keyhole of Lord Ashford's study.

Inside, Anthony was meeting with her father. She already knew that she would marry him even if her father followed through on his original threats to the contrary. She would still far rather that he agree, for she had no wish to be separated from her family, although Faith had made it clear she wouldn't listen to her father if he enforced such a rule.

"Lord Whitehall is telling Father that he would like to marry you," Faith whispered, then paused, pressing her ear harder against the door. They had agreed that she would be the one to listen as she had always had better hearing than Hope. "Now he is telling him that he has proof his father was not a traitor, proof that he is going to bring forward to the proper authorities as soon as Lord Ferrington delivers it."

Hope nodded, then saw Faith jump up when her eyes landed over Hope's shoulder. Hope turned to find her mother standing on the staircase behind them, but she waved them back toward the door.

"Keep listening," she instructed, and Hope and Faith exchanged a quick look of disbelief before Faith shrugged and did as her mother bade.

"Father is now saying that there are other gentlemen who have requested your hand, but that he was waiting to see if any might marry me first." Faith snorted and rolled her eyes. "None would, of course."

"Faith, do not say that. You—"

Faith waved away Hope's attempts to placate her. "Not to worry," she said. "I already knew this."

Her eyes then widened considerably, and Hope and her mother both leaned in against the door, all of them wanting to hear what had so startled Faith.

"I love her," Anthony's voice could be heard now, loud and resounding. "No other man will ever love her as I do. Which means that I will treat her better than any other man and will provide her with anything she desires in life."

There was a pause, and warmth spread through Hope's entire chest. He had said the words to her, yes, but the fact that he was sharing them with her father meant something else entirely.

"You are sincere," her father said, some surprise in his voice.

"Yes. I never say anything that I do not mean."

"What do you love about her?" her father asked, and Faith crinkled her nose, as though surprised he would ask. Hope also didn't quite believe it, but she was rather intrigued in Anthony's answer.

"What is there *not* to love about her?" Anthony said, more quietly now. "She is kind and considerate and puts everyone else before herself. She sees the good in every person and every situation. It can sometimes be difficult when she forgets about herself, but that is what I am there for. Well, me and Faith."

Faith chuckled lowly at that.

"She cannot stand to see injustice done," Anthony continued. "She makes me a better man. She loves with her entire heart. And she has more trust in her instincts than most other people I know."

There was a pause. "You never mentioned her beauty," her father said.

"Every other man wants her for her beauty and her lineage," Anthony said. "My reasons for wanting her are for all of the other reasons that no one else sees."

"You are sure that you can prove your father's innocence?"

"Yes," Anthony said.

"You will treat my daughter with the ultimate respect?"

"Yes," Anthony repeated.

"I cannot believe that I am saying this, but you are a stubborn man, Whitehall, and my wife is a willful woman. She has made it very clear that our daughter's happiness is of the utmost importance."

Faith and Hope exchanged a look before turning to their mother, who nodded approvingly. Lord Embury continued, "I know when to give up a fight. As long as I know my daughter will not be married to a traitor, then I will approve your union. As long as she agrees."

There was some humor in Anthony's voice now. "I am nearly certain she will."

They heard the rustling of fabric which was likely a handshake, and when footsteps and the tap of the cane Anthony had been using began toward the door, the three women scrambled back and away as quickly as they could.

"To the drawing room," their mother hissed, and they madly dashed toward it, having just sat down and properly arranged their skirts in a tableau when Hope's father and Anthony appeared.

Anthony looked at Hope knowingly, as though he was aware she had overheard the entirety of their conversation, but then his expression changed to a smile so loving that she nearly swooned right there at his feet.

"Hope," her father said gruffly. "Lord Whitehall here would like to speak with you."

Hope stood. "I think you might as well speak to all of us." After all, he had already asked her in private.

Her mother clapped her hands together just once before she lowered them into her lap, appearing contrite.

"Hope," Anthony said, crossing the room and taking her hands between his. "You know what you mean to me, and I promise to be the best man that I can be if you agree to be by my side. I will cherish you and put all of your needs first, if you will do me the honor of being my wife. Will you marry me?"

"Of course," she said, her smile matching his, as they held one another's gaze for a beat. She longed to lean in and kiss him, but she could hardly do so with her entire family watching. She would save that for later.

"Well," Faith said from across the room, as matter-of-fact as ever. "When is the wedding?"

"As soon as possible," Hope said, before noting the weariness in Anthony's eyes and leading him over to the sofa. He leaned on his cane as his ankle was still sore, but he had recovered a great deal in the past few days.

"Can we now finally return to Newfield Manor?" her father asked, and they nodded.

"I shall speak with my mother, but perhaps we should return with you until the wedding?" Anthony asked. "Then Hope can return home with me."

Hope squeezed his hand excitedly before she caught

Faith's expression. She was looking toward the floor now, masking the brief glimpse of pain there, and Hope knew what had caused it.

"We will not be far, Faith," she said, reaching out her other hand and clasping Faith's with it. "We shall visit so often."

"Of course," Anthony said. "You are welcome to stay with us anytime as well."

"And we shall likely be in London for the season, will we not?" Hope asked, turning to Anthony, who nodded.

"I do intend to continue to take my seat in Parliament."

"You see?" Hope said. "It will be like we are still together."

"Of course, Hope," Faith said with a smile that only Hope knew was forced. "I am ever so happy for you."

"We will have one more dinner tonight before we depart," their mother said. "And then we will finally return home."

* * *

ANTHONY'S HEAD still pounded now and again, but he thought he was doing a decent job of hiding it. The physician had told him that the only remedy to heal him was time, and it seemed he had progressed a great deal since the injury already. He was not, however, always a patient man. But Hope was now his, and that was all that mattered – well, nearly all.

He had just sat down at Castleton's dinner table, ready to suffer through another meal here, when Ashford entered with an envelope in his hand and a smile on his face.

"What has you so amused?" Anthony asked as the rest of the party joined them around the dining table. In addition to Hope's family and his mother, only Lord and Lady Covington also remained. Ashford's parents, the duke and duchess, were also present, taking their places near the head of the table.

"I have something I think you will be pleased about," Ashford said, taking his seat. "I know the dinner table is not the place for it, but I couldn't wait, and we will all want to hear this news."

Anthony lifted an eyebrow and waited.

"Ferrington sent the information he promised," he said. "The letters proving that Johnson was the traitor, including the fact that he set up your father."

"Are you certain?" Anthony asked, holding his breath, almost not wanting to believe it for fear that it might not be true.

"From what I can see, yes," he said. "We will have to take them to the army, but—"

"I can do it," Lord Embury said, surprising them. "I know who I can trust and can send it in confidence."

Anthony turned to him and met his eye. His future father-in-law nodded, telling him that he believed in him, that he was willing to put his name on the line for him.

Which meant more than he would likely ever realize.

"Thank you, Father." Hope beamed, her smile to be more valuable to Anthony than anything else in the world.

"I am glad that is resolved," Lord Ashford said as the footmen brought in the first course. "I know how much that weighed on you, Whitehall."

Anthony nodded, steepling his fingers together in front of him. Ashford's words were a bit of an understatement, but he appreciated the sentiment.

It wasn't until later in the evening, when the younger set was sitting around the card table playing a game of cribbage when Lord Ashford continued to reveal his plans.

"In other news," he continued, "I believe we need to speak to Aunt Eve."

"About the necklace?" Lady Covington asked, lifting her head, and Ashford nodded.

"I believe she is in possession of it."

"Will you ask her to send it?" Lady Covington asked, but her brother shook his head.

"She will likely only think we want it to sell it. While I would if I could, that isn't the case. I only need to inspect it, to see if the key were to fit within it. However, I have another plan."

His sister raised a brow in question.

"Rowley will be going to Bath."

"That's right," Anthony murmured.

"As Aunt Eve prefers to remain there, I will send the key with Rowley, and ask him to call upon her."

"Do you truly think she will allow a stranger in to see her most prized possession?" Lady Covington asked. "I can hardly see her agreeing to it."

"I'll send a note," Ashford said, but his sister was already shaking her head. "Do you have a better idea?"

"Actually," she said, "I do. Percy is also going to be in Bath."

"What difference does it make if your friend goes or mine?"

"Because Percy is a woman," Lady Covington said in exasperation. "Aunt Eve is far more likely to feel comfortable with her."

"I suppose," Ashford grumbled. "But I will send the key with Rowley. It will be easier to get it to him, and I would feel better about it being in his possession."

"You don't trust Percy?"

"That isn't it," he said. "We have seen what has happened to anyone searching for clues to this treasure before. I would rather Rowley be on the lookout than Lady Persephone."

"I suppose you are right," Lady Covington said. "I will

write to her and ask her to meet Mr. Rowley in Bath to call upon Aunt Eve."

"Very good."

"Now that that's decided," Lady Covington said with a smile, "we can move on to more important things." She turned to Hope and Anthony. "Such as just when will you be married?"

"As soon as we can," she said brightly with a smile, and Anthony nodded his agreement.

"I would like to return to my estate once we are married, as I'm hesitant to remain. I don't want Hope to be in any danger."

"You are the one who was shot at!" she exclaimed, but he shook his head.

"Still." He looked at Ashford. "If you need me to help with any additional codes or riddles, send me a message. And perhaps we can reconvene at our wedding. But I would rather not be in possession of anything that might put Hope in danger."

"Of course," Ashford said. "I understand."

"And if you ever discover who took a shot at me, do let me know, will you?"

"That I will."

Beneath the table, Hope placed her hand on Anthony's thigh, and he covered it with his own.

"Now," Lady Covington said, clearly interested in changing the subject, "whose turn is it next?"

EPILOGUE

*H*ope looked across the room at Anthony, seated so comfortably in the chair next to the fire. It was still hard to believe that she was Lady Whitehall.

He must have felt her stare upon him, for he looked up and met her eye.

"Is something wrong?" he asked with immediate concern.

"Not a thing," she said with a smile. "In fact, everything is very right."

Keeping the paper he had been reading in his hand, he walked across the room with a predatory look in his eyes. He stopped in front of her chair, crouching below it.

"I have something to show you."

"Do you now?" she said with a smirk, and he laughed.

"That too – but later. First," he held up the paper, "they have printed the story regarding Johnson's traitorous actions. And my father's own innocence."

"Oh, Anthony," she said, picking it up in her hands. "That is wonderful."

"It is," he said with a sigh. "It is all over."

"You will have to write to Reeves, in case he hasn't seen it."

"I will. He will be pleased. Although I'm not sure anyone will be as happy as my mother was to hear of it. I knew it had weighed on her but hadn't realized quite how much."

"In other news, I've heard from Percy," she said. "She is to meet Mr. Rowley this week and they are going to call upon Cassandra's Aunt Eve."

"Oh, good," Anthony said absently. "Rowley's a good man. A smart one, too. He'll know what to do."

"Do you think he can keep Percy safe?"

"That, I'm not sure," he admitted. "But he would most certainly try. He is quite chivalrous."

"He is."

"Percy is inquisitive, if nothing else," Hope said. "But enough of that."

She stood, placing her hands on Anthony's arms and sitting him down in the chair, then sat in his lap and looped her arms around his neck.

"Are you happy?" he asked her, and she smiled wide.

"Do I look happy?"

"Yes. But you always do."

"There is so much good to life," she said. "Especially when I have you."

"If there is one thing I am glad of," he said, "it is that I broke the code of how to have you."

"That is where you are wrong," she said, tapping him on the nose. "For I believe *you* were the code most difficult to break."

"You might be right about that," he said sheepishly. "It took me far too long to discover the cipher I needed to solve what was missing in my life was you."

"But you did," she said, leaning in and placing her lips against his. "That's what matters most."

"I love you, Hope."

"And I love you, Anthony."

"Will you play for me?" he asked, and she smiled.

"Of course," she said, sliding off his lap and holding a hand out toward him. "But only if you accompany me."

He accepted her offered hand and followed her over to the pianoforte, taking a seat beside her. Yes, her music brought peace to his soul, but she had also given him another gift – a reminder of the love he had for song, how partaking himself brought him as much joy as her voice did.

Perhaps he would never be the same as he was before his father died. But he could remember the best parts of him and be the man he wanted to be.

As he opened his mouth and joined with Hope in song, he was also reminded that a little light and a little love could go a long way.

And he would never let that melody go again.

THE END

* * *

Dear reader,

I hope you have enjoyed the second book of the Reckless Rogues! Wondering where the next clue leads to? You can follow the treasure trail and discover what comes next in The Scholar's Key, a second son, friends-to-lovers, makeover story featuring Percy and Noah.

In the meantime, if you enjoyed this story and are looking for a completed series to read, I would recommend The Remingtons of the Regency, starting with The Mystery of the Debonair Duke.

And if you haven't yet signed up for my newsletter, I would

love to have you join! You will receive a free book, as well as links to giveaways, sales, new releases, and stories about my coffee addiction, my struggle to keep my plants alive, and how much trouble one loveable wolf-lookalike dog can get into.

www.elliestclair.com/ellies-newsletter

Or you can join my Facebook group, Ellie St. Clair's Ever Afters, and stay in touch daily.

With love,
Ellie

* * *

The Scholar's Key
Reckless Rogues Book 3

LADY PERSEPHONE HOLLOWAY **is determined to avoid a loveless arranged marriage – she just doesn't realize that the Prince Charming she's been searching for might be closer than she thinks.**

Mr. Noah Rowley, second son of an earl, finally knows what he wants. A career in banking, and Lady Percy. Only one, however, seems like a dream that might come true. For his unrequited love sees him as a friend, and he knows better than to ever wish for more.

Drawn together in Bath as they attempt to solve a clue on their treasure hunt, Percy convinces Mr. Rowley to let her make him over to charm his way into recovering a stolen item. The biggest surprise, however, is her own reaction to Mr. Rowley himself, sparking new emotions that threaten to shatter any chance of a happy ending.

Mr. Rowley must now decide if it is worth risking it all or remain forever in his unrequited love.

This is a friends-to-lovers, opposites attract, ugly-duckling-turned-swan, unrequited love Regency romance featuring a plucky heroine and a secretly intriguing hero. The Reckless Rogues series is best read in order.

THE SCHOLAR'S KEY -
CHAPTER ONE

*L*ady Persephone Holloway hated weddings.

This one, however, was an exception.

Most weddings she attended were the finalization of a contract, one that hardly involved the bride and groom themselves. Instead, two people who barely knew one another were tied together in the hopes that they might create a life together. One in which the husband could go ahead and do as he pleased, while the wife was to obey him for all of her days.

No, thank you.

This wedding, blessedly, was different. It was celebrating the love of two people who were choosing to be together because they couldn't imagine a life apart.

That was a wonderful story, and one that she could support.

Especially when the bride was one of her closest friends.

"She is beautiful," Percy whispered in Faith's ear. Faith sat stoically watching the proceedings, and Percy wondered if her friend was actually seeing the event in front of her, for she was barely blinking. "Faith, are you all right?"

Faith nodded, although her jaw was set so tightly that Percy was worried for her teeth.

"She will always be part of your life, you know," she said again. "She will never truly leave you."

Faith nodded again, and Percy leaned over and squeezed her hand. She knew that while Faith was happy for her sister, Hope's marriage also meant that Faith would no longer have her sister by her side. If only Faith would be open to marriage herself. But, it seemed, that was not to be.

Percy leaned into say something else to Faith, but stopped suddenly when she sensed she was being watched. She looked up to find Mr. Noah Rowley's eyes on her, his brow furrowed behind his spectacles, his mouth in a grim line as he appeared disapproving. Percy slunk back in her seat, feeling properly chastised, an uneasy swirl in her stomach.

Very well, then. If the scholarly Mr. Rowley felt that she should be silent, then silent she would be.

She would never admit that actually sitting back and observing the rest of the ceremony was lovely. Hope, with her soft features, golden blond hair and perfect curves looked like an angel up front, contrasting rather wonderfully with Lord Whitehall, as dark featured and surly as Hope was radiant.

It was, however, the happiest Percy had ever seen the viscount.

When the wedding was over, they all made the short journey to Newfield Manor, where the wedding breakfast awaited them. It was a loud event, with all of the chattering amongst the guests, none louder than Hope's mother. Percy had always been rather fond of Lady Newfield, despite the fact that she never stopped talking. At least there were never awkward silences when she was present.

Cassandra, the new Lady Covington, was sitting to Percy's right during the breakfast, and when everyone was otherwise engaged listening to a story Lord Ferrington was telling about the last horse race he had attended, Cassandra tugged on Percy's elbow to gain her attention.

"Percy, you know that we have determined where the next clue is leading us."

"Of course," Percy said. Cassandra had stumbled upon a riddle that was tucked inside the pages of a book from her family's estate. She had shared it with the other four of them who made up their secretive book club, and they had decided to embark on solving its secrets.

As it happened, Cassandra's brother, Lord Ashford and the future Duke of Sheffield, had found a duplicate copy and he and his four closest friends had done the same. Of course, it had all ended well for Cassandra as she had fallen in love with Lord Covington, except that the riddle hadn't led them to a treasure but rather the next clue.

It was Hope and Lord Whitehall, who had learned from his father how to break codes, who had solved the next. They had discovered a key that they were sure would fit into a necklace set that belonged to Cassandra's family.

The necklace, however, was with Cassandra's aunt.

"We need to reunite the key and the necklace. I don't know how, but the necklace is part of this. Since you are going to Bath…"

"You would like me to visit your aunt."

"Yes, if you would?" Cassandra said, her expression so earnest that even if Percy had been inclined to say no – which of course she wasn't – she never could have.

"I'll arrange for you to have it before we leave Newfield," Cassandra said.

After they had eaten, Percy wandered away to the drawing room window, taking her drink with her as she looked out at the sea stretching beyond. Newfield was situated on the coast near Harwich, and she wished she had more time to spend here and appreciate the beautiful landscape.

"Are you not having fun?"

Percy turned to find her mother standing behind her, her brow arched. Her mother was a rather quiet woman, yet not in an introverted manner. Rather, when she spoke it was with care that every word had meaning, and she was as curious as Percy about the world around her, although in a much more observant and unobtrusive way.

"Of course I am," Percy said, smiling fondly at her mother. "I was just taking a moment to myself."

Her mother turned and surveyed the room behind them. It primarily included Hope's family and their close friends. "There are many unmarried young men here," she said, before they turned back to face the window.

"So there are," Percy remarked, sipping her drink.

"Are there none that you might be interested in? You have been spending a great deal of time with this crowd."

"Yes, but—"

She was about to say why she had seen them so frequently – because they had come together to solve a riddle which was leading them down a long and winding path of a treasure hunt. One that was likely to come to nothing but was rather fun to participate in, nonetheless. As it was, Percy now had her own role in the hunt that she was quite excited about.

"It is because Cassandra so recently married her brother's friend. It has brought our circles together."

"I see," her mother said. "Well, there is a certain earl, as well as a future duke among them."

"I am not interested in Cassandra's brother," Percy said, nearly rolling her eyes. She liked Lord Ashford, but he was far from being a strong enough man for her. Percy knew that she wasn't the shy, fair lady that most men sought out. She was still looking for a man who would match her wit for wit, who would challenge her, question her – and she wouldn't be opposed a man who could lift her up and throw her on the bed.

Perhaps she had been reading too many scandalous romantic novels.

"As it is, none of the men here are who I am looking for," she continued.

"Percy," her mother's face softened. "You know I only want what is best for you."

"And getting married is what is best," Percy finished.

"It is how it is."

"You said I could choose my husband."

"And you can," her mother said. "But you are already two and twenty, and—"

"And I am running out of time. I know."

Her mother smiled kindly. "Your father is becoming rather impatient, but I am doing my best to keep him happy. He does, however, have a man in mind."

Percy frowned. "He does, does he?"

"Yes. You know his friend, Lord Lecher?"

"Yeeees…"

"He has a son, Lord Stephen, who will be titled one day."

"I remember him. He tormented me when we visited them years ago."

"Well, he is grown up now, and is quite handsome, I am told."

A clattering behind them had them both jumping, and Percy turned around, surprised when she saw Mr. Rowley bent over, his drink spilled over the ground, the glass shattered into pieces.

"Goodness," she said, bending down to help him. "Are you all right?"

"Fine," he said. "My apologies. Lady Fairfax," he said, tilting his head downward in deference to her mother.

"I shall go find a footman," Percy's mother said, walking away, leaving the two of them together.

Percy reached out to help him with the glass pieces, her hand hitting his when she did – causing a jolt to zing up her arm. She was shocked at first – surely Mr. Rowley wouldn't cause such a reaction within her – but then she saw the blood drip onto the floor and realized it wasn't caused by Mr. Rowley at all.

It was from the piece of glass she had cut her finger on.

~~~~~

"Lady Persephone, you are hurt!" Noah swore at himself. Not only had he been listening to her conversation with her mother, as much as he had tried not to, but then he had clumsily dropped his glass and Lady Percy had injured herself trying to help him.

For an intelligent man, he could be such an idiot.

"It's fine," she said, sucking her finger into her mouth, causing an unwelcome surge of lust to plunge straight to his groin. "Do you, perhaps, have a handkerchief?"

"Of course," he said, reaching into a jacket for one, which she accepted with a smile. While Lady Hope was known to be a beauty, he still thought Lady Persephone Holloway was the most intriguing woman he had ever seen.

And she, in turn, didn't even see him, except as the brother of an earl who was friends with her friend's brother. Hardly an acquaintance. Until he had injured her.

"I took off my gloves to eat," she said, a small smile on her face. "I should have returned them."

"It would have saved your finger, yes," he said, unable to meet her eye. "Do you need someone to tend to you?"

"It should be fine, once it stops bleeding. I have likely ruined your handkerchief, however, even though I asked for it." She laughed, a long, loud laugh that warmed his soul. "I am horrible."

"Not at all."

Far from it, in fact.

No, Lady Persephone was beautiful, vibrant, inquisitive, and everything that Noah could ever admire in a woman.

And, judging from the conversation he had accidentally overheard, she was not aware that he was even in the room. She hadn't even seen to mention him to her mother when telling her all of the reasons why she was uninterested in any of the men within. And as for the ideal man she described? Noah was the exact opposite.

"Were you coming to speak with me?"

"Pardon?" Noah said, beginning to inwardly panic.

"You were right behind me when you dropped the glass."

Right. The truth was, he was taking a moment to himself in the corner of the room, and then Lady Percy and her mother had begun talking on the other side of the potted plant. He hadn't wanted them to think that he was listening on purpose, and so hadn't made his escape until their conversation became so personal that he was feeling far too guilty for listening in.

Then his glass had fallen.

"Ah, yes, I was coming to speak to you," he lied, his thoughts beginning to make sense in his head. "I have heard that we are both going to be in Bath soon. Gideon – Lord Ashford – has asked me to pay a visit to his aunt, and he has told me that Cassandra has asked you to do the same."

"She has?" Lady Percy said, surprise on her face. "Do they not trust me, then?"

"I do not think that is it," Noah said quickly. "Perhaps they believe we are best to work together."

"Perhaps," Lady Percy said, although she didn't look convinced. "What takes you to Bath?"

Noah smiled, enjoying this time with her. He wasn't sure he had ever had the opportunity to speak with her one-on-one before.

"Actually—"

"Noah, there you are."

Noah sighed at the voice of his brother. He loved the man more than anyone else in the world, but sometimes he truly had the worst timing.

"Lady Persephone, you look as beautiful as always."

Her pink lips tipped upward in a smile that met her eyes as one of her red-gold curls bobbed down over her temple.

"Thank you, Lord Ferrington. You look quite dashing yourself. You both do," she said, including Noah in her compliment, although he was aware that she was only doing so to be polite.

"You are too kind," his brother said, as charming as ever, and as Lady Percy's attention shifted toward Eric, Noah was reminded that even if Lady Percy wasn't interested in her brother, he was, and always would be, the favored one of the two of them.

And it was best that he never forget it, or else the only thing he was going to be was sorely disappointed.

* * *

FIND THE SCHOLAR'S Key on Amazon and in Kindle Unlimited!

ALSO BY ELLIE ST. CLAIR

The Duke She Wished For

Someday Her Duke Will Come

Once Upon a Duke's Dream

He's a Duke, But I Love Him

Loved by the Viscount

Because the Earl Loved Me

Happily Ever After Box Set Books 1-3

Happily Ever After Box Set Books 4-6

The Victorian Highlanders

Duncan's Christmas - (prequel)

Callum's Vow

Finlay's Duty

Adam's Call

Roderick's Purpose

Peggy's Love

The Victorian Highlanders Box Set Books 1-5

Searching Hearts

Duke of Christmas (prequel)

Quest of Honor

Clue of Affection

Hearts of Trust

Hope of Romance

Promise of Redemption

Searching Hearts Box Set (Books 1-5)

Christmas

Christmastide with His Countess

Her Christmas Wish

Merry Misrule

A Match Made at Christmas

A Match Made in Winter

Standalones

Always Your Love

The Stormswept Stowaway

A Touch of Temptation

For a full list of all of Ellie's books, please see
<u>www.elliestclair.com/books</u>.

ABOUT THE AUTHOR

 Ellie has always loved reading, writing, and history. For many years she has written short stories, non-fiction, and has worked on her true love and passion -- romance novels.

In every era there is the chance for romance, and Ellie enjoys exploring many different time periods, cultures, and geographic locations. No matter when or where, love can always prevail. She has a particular soft spot for the bad boys of history, and loves a strong heroine in her stories.

Ellie and her husband love nothing more than spending time at home with their children and Husky cross. Ellie can typically be found at the lake in the summer, pushing the stroller all year round, and, of course, with her computer in her lap or a book in hand.

She also loves corresponding with readers, so be sure to contact her!

www.elliestclair.com
ellie@elliestclair.com

Ellie St. Clair's Ever Afters Facebook Group

Printed in Great Britain
by Amazon

39198030R00138